DEMON SUMMONED

SKYE MALONE

Demon Summoned
Book Two of the Demon Guardians Series
by Skye Malone

Previously Published as
DESIRE ME: Book Two of the Demon Guardians Series

Copyright 2017 - Skye Malone
Published by Wildflower Isle | P.O. Box 129, Savoy, IL 61874
www.wildflowerisle.com

ISBN: 978-1-940617-76-3

Library of Congress Control Number: 2017933034

Cover design by Karri Klawiter
www.artbykarri.com

Proofreading by Monica Bogza
www.trustedaccomplice.com

Find out about all new releases:
Join Skye Malone's mailing list at skyemalone.com/mailinglist!

AUTHOR'S NOTE

This book was previously published as
DESIRE ME: Book Two of the Demon Guardians Series.

If you have already read Desire Me, then you have already
read this book.

NEW RELEASES, GIVEAWAYS, AND MORE!

Be the first to hear about all the great sales and giveaways when you join Skye Malone's exclusive mailing list!

Go online today to skyemalone.com/mailinglist to join in!

1

"Who are you?" I demand, staring at the enormous, bald man in the doorway of Bianca's penthouse apartment. He hasn't stopped smiling since he came in here, and his metal teeth glint in the firelight.

It's terrifying. I manage to keep my voice from shaking when I speak, but I can't stop the shivers running through me at the sight of his cyborg-from-hell smile.

He chuckles. "The name's Ram. Like, battering ram?" He looks at Amar and Bianca. "You figure out why."

I glance at them warily.

"He's a troll," Amar explains to me without taking his eyes from the guy.

My mouth moves, working to find a reply. A troll? I've already learned that vampires are real. Werewolves too. And let's not forget me, the girl who discovered she is half *succubus* not too long ago, thanks to my biological mom, who I've never met.

But a troll? *Seriously*?

A tiny sound escapes my best friend, Ruby, at Amar's

words. A human in a room full of demons—me, included —she hasn't moved from her spot on the couch, where she's been since we rescued her from the fight to the death that a bunch of kidnapping bastards had planned for her only a short while ago. Bianca's two Dobermans stand growling at my friend's side, radiating protectiveness and a full willingness to rip out this guy's throat.

"You were watching us," Amar continues to the man. "By the river and then at the set last night. Are you with Volgert? Another House?"

Ram's grin doesn't fade. "She knows I'm not." He jerks his chin at me.

I blink, lost. How am I supposed to know that?

"You think it was an accident I knew about that explosion at the set before it happened?" Ram continues. "You know, the one that tore up the gate in that hellhole where the House Volgert scum had this girl?" He nods toward Ruby. "Your wolves were getting slaughtered back there. You didn't stand a chance of reaching her till we helped."

I don't respond. He had known, though. He'd looked right at the gate before it blew up.

"That explosion crushed half the cages in there," Amar says. "It could have killed the girl."

"Not a chance. We knew what side of the room they were keeping the Touched on."

"Enough," Bianca snaps. A full-blood succubus with an attitude to match, she glares at the man while magic tangles like electrified pink fog around her fists, and the air crackles with static in response. "What the hell do you want?"

"Just to deliver a message to Cait." Ram returns his attention to me. "House Linden's already got their eye on you. Volgert and all the other Houses are going to start circling too, now that you've shown your face at that set and given all of them a good look at you. And if you are who we *think* you are, there's a lot you need to know if you plan to survive that interest. So let us help you. Come meet us. Boris and Sons Salvage Yard. Tomorrow after sunset."

What? If I am who they think I am? "Come—" It's hard to keep my voice from shaking this time. "Come meet who?"

Ram doesn't answer the question. His eyes flick over to Amar and his lip twitches, disgust heavy in the expression. "Be careful who you trust," he tells me.

Without another word, he turns and heads out the door.

"Hey!" Bianca snaps, striding toward the entryway after him. "What the hell do you—"

"Bianca," Amar says.

She stops, and he shakes his head at her slightly. Bianca stares for a second and then turns away, muttering a curse while she marches to the side table and snatches up her cell phone. In only a moment, she's rapid-firing orders at someone on the other end and giving them hell for letting Ram inside in the first place.

Amar comes over to me. "You okay?"

"What was *that*?" I whisper desperately.

He doesn't respond, his attention on Bianca.

"'If I am who they think I am'?" I press. "What was he talking about? And what was with that look he gave you?"

"I don't know."

"Do you think he works for Linden?"

He's silent.

"Amar?"

"Bianca's people will find out."

I glance at the girl. She's still furious—I can tell that

from across the room—but it seems like she's getting actual information too.

"Okay," I allow. "But—"

"Cait." Amar twitches his head toward Ruby.

I falter. Right. Ruby. My best friend who just watched a damn *troll* show up. And that's after everything else she's been through with the Houses and their death match and nearly losing her mind to magic because they turned her into one of the Touched.

She's so much more important right now.

I nod quickly, dropping my questions. Amar follows while I hurry over to the couch.

"Are you all right?" I ask her, sinking down nearby.

Ruby's eyes slide toward me and then away. I wince. Stupid question.

"I-I'm sorry about all that," I try. "We're safe here, though. I promise." I work to put as much belief as I can into the words, hoping they're true. "Is there anything I can get for you? Water? Something to eat?"

Her head shakes, a faint motion. I look to Amar for help.

"How, um…" Ruby whispers, her voice rough and shaky. "How long was I, um…"

"Twenty-four hours," Amar replies quietly. "It's been about twenty-four hours since they took you."

A ragged breath leaves Ruby, like a laugh that might, at any moment, become a sob. Her brow twitches down like she's trying to figure out how to process the words.

"Nothing that happened during that time was your fault," Amar continues. "You're not responsible for what they did to you or whatever came as a result."

Ruby's gaze quivers toward him, like she's not sure if she should trust the words.

Or maybe just their source.

"What, um…" Her voice is a whisper as her focus darts to me and then back to him. "What are you?"

I search for an answer, glancing at Amar. He raises an eyebrow at me, the expression gentle but, nonetheless, making it clear he's decided that whatever we tell her is my call.

I can't quite be grateful. I'm too busy feeling nauseated.

Clearing my throat, I brace myself. "We're, um—"

Ruby's attention snaps to me, her eyes widening with alarm, and my stomach climbs my throat. Oh. Oh God, she was asking about him, not me.

I scramble for a way to explain.

"Cait's human," Amar offers into the silence. "Mostly."

Ruby hasn't stopped staring at me, but her brow climbs higher at the statement.

"I-I'm sorry." My words come out choked. "I didn't know till a few days ago."

She looks away and pulls the blanket tighter around herself. "I want to go back to the apartment now."

Shit. "Um, yeah. About that…"

"Your place is a wreck," Amar fills in when I trail off. "The demons trashed it after they took you, to make it look like a robbery gone wrong. There's nowhere to sleep. It'd be better if you stayed here for the time being."

For a moment, Ruby doesn't react, and I don't know what to do. There isn't anywhere safer than this. Not really. Amar's apartment maybe, but—

Ruby gives a jerky nod and pushes away from the couch, not looking at either of us.

Across the room, Bianca hangs up the phone. With a quick glance between us all, she seems to read the situation. "This way." She motions toward the stairs. "You can use one of the guest rooms. Shower's down the hall if you want that too."

Ruby nods again. The Dobermans trail her across the room and up the steps.

I want to follow her. Find some way to explain.

I have no idea where to begin.

"Give her time," Amar says.

I nod for lack of anything else to do. I hope time fixes this. I'm scared to death it won't.

She looked at me like I was a *monster*.

"Cait."

I exhale sharply, pushing the thought away. "Yeah?"

"One other thing."

An incredulous noise threatens to escape me, and I barely hold it inside. There's something *else* now? "What?"

Amar hesitates. "Ruby. Chances are… there will be side effects."

My stomach twists. Oh. That. Bianca had started to say something about that right before that troll guy showed up.

I brace myself, not really wanting to hear it and knowing I have to anyway.

"I don't think she's noticed it yet, but…" Amar grimaces. "It's not common for people to be saved after they become one of the Touched. Most don't come back."

I nod tightly. Bianca's brother, Brett, told me that earlier —how only about five percent of the Touched ever manage to recover. But Ruby had. I'd hoped that was the end of it.

"The ones who can be saved, though," Amar continues. "They have side effects—and I don't just mean the memories. You remember how I told you she could tell what you were, back when you first saw her at the set?"

I remember what she looked like, desperately clawing

for us through the bars of a cage, her green eyes wild. I wish I could forget. "Yeah."

"Things changed in her when Volgert's people hooked her on the mist. She's still going to be sensitive to it. To magic in others."

"Like she's still addicted?"

"Not necessarily. But Ruby also can't go back to the way she was. She'll still be able to feel that magic inside people. You, me, Bianca. Others too, like werewolves or vampires. Everyone in the demonic world has something that separates us from humans. Depending on how sensitive she ends up being, she might be able to detect it in all of us."

"Okay, but that's not exactly—"

"Some of us don't like to be recognized for what we are, Cait. Pretty much all of us, actually. And while it might annoy a few… others will kill over it."

Oh.

I inhale sharply, attempting to stay calm. "What do I do?"

Amar pauses. "We. What do we do."

I look up at him. His eyebrow rises slightly. I swallow hard. "Yeah."

"We protect her. In any way we can."

For a second, I can't take my eyes off him. It's so simple, those statements, and right now they sort of mean the world to me. I'm not alone in this. I never have been. And neither is Ruby.

I tense, fighting the impulse to reach out to him. I know that here, at Bianca's, the motion probably won't be welcome. Demons don't do affection. Hell, they barely do kindness.

"Hey." Bianca's voice shatters the moment, almost as if

proving my point. "Your friend's got the guest room at the end of the hall," she says, coming down the stairs. "You can have the other one if you want. Till you get your place cleaned up, anyway."

I nod. Some part of me wishes I could stay at Amar's, but that'd probably be hard to explain to Bianca's satisfaction. Even if I don't really know what this thing is between Amar and me, Bianca would be disgusted at the merest hint that there was anything else going on besides the strategic value of helping a fellow neutral.

Anyway, I can't leave Ruby here alone.

"Thanks," I tell Bianca.

She shrugs like she couldn't care less and then disappears into the kitchen.

"You need anything," Amar says to me, his voice low, "I'll be down here."

I nod again and reluctantly walk toward the stairs.

2

AMAR

By the wall of windows in Bianca's apartment, he stands, watching the dead streets and the lonely stoplights that flash for no one. A cool breeze from the air conditioner brushes his bare torso and stirs against the cotton pants he keeps here for whenever he stays over. His gaze glides back and forth across the empty sidewalks, as restless as he had been when he abandoned any pretense of sleep among the blankets on the couch. He tracks a stray dog slipping out of an alleyway, a bat flitting past a lamp in a blur of quick shadow.

And he tries not to think about how, in the space of a few short days, his life has torn itself apart.

For her.

His mouth tightens briefly, a hint of expression, all he allows himself. He hadn't intended this. Hadn't meant to seek it out, that night at the oh-so-ironically-named Temptation. But Cait had been such a mystery, running like she had. Helping that Touched girl as she did. And when he found out she was a Legacy… an inexplicable, impossible *new* Legacy, who somehow never knew of her demon half, who never destroyed her own humanity for the sake of survival in the demonic world…

It didn't matter. He still should have walked away. He'd been smarter than this, once.

His eyes fasten on a couple walking along the street. They're too far away for him to judge by their body language if they're ordinary humans. The distance won't matter for Ruby, though. Not once she gets past her own horror and becomes aware of what's happened to her.

There'd been a time he might have considered using that, or at least wouldn't have stopped Bianca or Brett from doing the same. But now…

The couple rounds the corner and disappears from view.

Letting out a breath, he turns away from the tall windows. He knows what it is. Why he hadn't abandoned Cait at the start. Why he keeps compromising every rule that's kept him safe, no matter how suicidal that compromise could prove to be. By this point, most Legacies like him knew they lived on a knife's edge, always in danger of looking not enough like predators and too much like prey. They'd long since eradicated every trace of what they'd once been in an unending quest to become indistinguishable from the demons with whom they'd never *truly* belong. And to allow anyone to see that the human side of you wasn't fully dead…

It meant taking your life in your hands.

Until her.

His eyes close briefly. He knows he needs to get his emotions back under control, but she's made it harder. He keeps letting down his guard with her. Keeps getting caught by the sheer wonder of her, the only person he's ever seen who might accept both sides of him. Who isn't revolted by his humanity, who wasn't terrified to find out he's a demon. And who looks at him with those deep, gorgeous hazel eyes like she wants—*desperately* wants—to know and trust the person he secretly hopes he still is somewhere inside.

It's breathtaking. Liberating. Excruciating.

And it tells him lies.

He rests a hand on the back of a stiff armchair. He can't lose himself to this, to any of it. Bianca is still a problem, and he's certain she'll see through him eventually. He's amazed, on some level, that she hasn't already. He convinced her that he only wanted to help Cait because she could be useful to him; one more neutral Legacy with whom to form an alliance. He made her believe that was the end of it.

There's no predicting what Bianca will do when she realizes he lied to her.

And worse are the other demons. It makes him sick to think they might suspect he cares for Cait, sick to think what they might *do* in response to that knowledge. Emotion was leverage, after all, and pain was too. But then, his actions thus far have been explainable. They've had strategic value.

Except for the ones that ended him up at the set last night.

And what he did while there…

His fingers press into the white upholstery. Cait won't have to know. Last night will be the end of it. The closest he's come in years to the nightmare of what he is, and the closest he'll *need* to come. It's over now.

He runs his gaze over the silhouetted furniture and décor of the apartment, working to believe the thought.

The shadows are thick here; more than bulletproof glass impedes the moonlight trying to illuminate the room. Defenses coat the apartment, set in place from the moment the daughter of business mogul Milford Chastain moved in, and reinforced often by the army of personal security Bianca keeps on the floors below. They shouldn't have broken for anyone, not even a troll.

If she is who they think she is…

The words haunt him. He fears what they might mean. He'd hoped Cait was simply a castoff. The child of some demon who hadn't been able to locate her for one reason or another—as unlikely as that might be. He'd tried to make himself believe that Volgert's strange fixation on her and the way Alistair Linden looked at her could all be chalked up to their desire to conscript another succubus to their cause.

But now…

Slowly, he draws in air. It doesn't matter. Volgert, Linden, whoever the hell that troll is working for… they don't matter. He'll still protect her. Himself too. There has to be a finish line to this, an exit that will allow Cait to live outside the Houses and their hell. After all, he'd made it out when no one believed he could. He'll help her do the same.

Somehow.

A noise comes from the second floor, soft and scarcely more than a whimper, and instantly, his tumultuous thoughts are gone. With a sweep of his eyes to the windows, he confirms there is nothing but an empty street outside, and then he strides toward the stairs.

3

I SNAP BACK TO CONSCIOUSNESS, AND I DON'T KNOW WHY.

Eyes wide, I stare around the darkened room, ghosts of nightmares blurring my vision. I'm too hot beneath the white duvet on the massive California-king bed, and for a moment, all the shadows cast by the moonlight look like people looming over me.

The hairs on my arms stand on end, static crackling over my skin. I shove the blanket away and bolt upright.

Shadows become furniture and art. No one is in the room but me.

A shuddering breath leaves my chest as I struggle to get my magic under control. The last thing I need is Bianca yelling because I've accidentally blown up something in her apartment again.

It's difficult. My heart is still pounding. Lingering sweat from my nightmare chills me and makes my skin pebble in the cool air. I'd been dreaming about Volgert's set, only this time, it was Amar down in that pit, bleeding to death while I couldn't do anything but watch.

Scrubbing a hand over my face, I try to push the memory away. I don't know what woke me up, but I'm grateful something did.

A choked cry comes from the next room, killing my gratitude.

Ruby.

Scrambling from the bed, I rush to the door. The t-shirt Bianca lent me hangs to my thighs, while the pajama shorts do little to cover the rest of my legs. I tug open the door, only to freeze when I see Amar at the end of the darkened hallway. He's shirtless, dressed only in loose cotton pants. Despite my alarm at the noise I heard, the sight still makes my heart race for a whole new reason.

He comes toward me. "Are you okay?" he whispers, his voice barely audible.

"Wasn't me," I whisper back.

The sound comes again, more like a sob this time. I hurry toward the guest room at the end of the hall, and the door makes no noise when I edge it open. "Ruby?"

She twists under the bedsheets like she's fighting something, but her eyes are closed tight. I scan the room fast. No one else is here.

Amar's hand comes to rest on my arm. I jump.

"Do you—" he starts.

I shake my head. "Just give me a second." I cross the room to her side. "Ruby?" I take her shoulder. "Ru—"

She lunges awake with a strangled cry, her fists swinging as if to drive me away. I retreat fast.

Eyes wide, she stares at me. "Cait?" Relief flashes across her face, and then suddenly, it's swallowed up in fear. Her focus darts from me to the door where I know Amar is waiting.

I glance at him. I don't know what he sees on my face,

but after a heartbeat, he simply nods. Without a word, he shuts the door, leaving me alone with Ruby.

"What are you doing here?" she whispers.

I look back only to falter. She's scared of me. My best friend in the whole world, and she looks absolutely *terrified* of me. "You were having a nightmare."

She shifts on the bed like she's trying to escape. "O-okay, well…"

"Ruby, I'm not a monster."

The words blurt out. I clamp my mouth shut to keep anything else from emerging—like maybe a plea that she'll stop looking at me that way.

She draws the blanket closer as if it's a shield between us. "Are you like him?"

"Who? Amar?"

Her expression tightens, unwilling and angry at the same time. "Kyle."

I'm not sure what to say. That sick Volgert bastard who kidnapped her is a Legacy too; a half-blood like me, like Amar. He told me so after he took Ruby. But Kyle and I are not the same. Not remotely.

I have no idea how to explain that. "Not… not exactly. I—"

"Then what are you?"

I search for an answer. One that doesn't involve the words demon or succubus. "They, uh… they call what I am a Legacy. It's like, half, um, half human and half… not."

"Your birth mom."

"Yeah." I hesitate. "I don't know much beyond that."

It's mostly true. I know practically nothing—except for the fact my biological mother was a succubus, anyway.

"And these people?" Her eyes twitch toward the rest of the apartment illustratively.

"They're good. I mean, Bianca's kind of a bitch, but… they helped me save you. I met them a few days ago when —" I hedge fast around the details. "—when some weird stuff started happening."

"Weird stuff?" She watches me distrustfully.

"I-it's hard to describe. It's not—"

"You didn't like Kyle. That day when we all had lunch at the café, you seemed… freaked."

My mouth moves. I hate this conversation. It's not cooperating, and it's going to end me up saying things that will make Ruby even more afraid of me than before. "Something seemed off about him."

"Did you know what he—that he was going to—"

"No. I *swear* to you, no. Not—"

I look away fast, slamming my mouth shut all over again. I don't know how to explain. I *should* have known. Or at least done more. I knew demons could break Protections, after all. For pity's sake, only about a week ago I helped a girl who'd had that done to her. So I should have—

"Not what?" she asks.

I close my eyes, a blur of cursing running through my mind.

"Cait?"

The trepidation in her voice is terrible.

"Kyle found me later," I say. "Threatened you."

A shaky breath leaves her. "Why would Kyle tell *you* a threat against *me*?"

"He thinks I'm involved in something, but I'm not."

Ruby stares at me. "And *that's* why he did this to me? Why he… he—"

She turns away sharply, shaking like she's fighting the urge to scream or cry.

I flounder, desperate for something to say. *Anything* to say that'll bring that horrified look in her eyes to an end. I can't even imagine what she saw or went through after that bastard shattered the Protection spells Amar put around her as a favor to me.

But I'd seen the result. She'd barely been human, reduced to a raving, magic-addicted animal covered in bloodstains.

Ones from whomever she'd killed.

"I'm sorry, Ruby. I'm so, *so* sorry. I tried to stop them and keep you safe, I swear I did, but—"

"Don't." She holds up a hand, not meeting my eyes. "Just… don't."

I can't even move while I wait to hear what she's going to say.

"I need sleep," she continues in the same tense voice. "I just… I need to…"

She doesn't move, her hand still raised and her eyes on some middle point between us like she can't even bring herself to look at me.

It hurts. God, it hurts.

"O-okay," I manage. "I, um… Right."

I shift my feet, feeling suddenly like I take up too much space in this otherwise ridiculously large guest room. Uncomfortably, I retreat to the door, only to pause with my hand on the handle.

"I'm sorry," I say again. "I swear, Ruby. I'm so sorry."

I flee the room.

⌖

Amar is waiting outside. "What happened?"

I don't even know where to begin. "She blames me."

"She what?"

I look away. Maybe that was an exaggeration. Maybe *I* just blamed me. But it felt pretty close to the truth.

"Cait—"

I shake my head, cutting him off. "Please, I—"

I bolt back to the other guest room. I can't handle this. The way she'd looked at me. The way she *hadn't*. I need to wake up and have it be Friday again, before Kyle and House Volgert took her. Before I'd failed to protect my best friend from the monsters, and then things had gone even *more* to hell.

My feet come to a stop by the bed. I don't want to lie down. I don't want to sleep again and revisit those nightmares. I can barely close my eyes without seeing that pit or Kyle's horrible grin after he kidnapped Ruby or that troll with his glistening teeth.

So many monsters. How did my life become filled with *so* many monsters?

The door shuts. I don't turn back. Air stirs when Amar walks up behind me.

"It's not your fault," he says gently. I shift my shoulders against the words. His hands come to rest on me, stilling the motion. "It's not."

I don't respond. He turns me around to face him. I can feel him studying me, though I can't meet his eyes.

He sighs. His grip moves, dropping from my shoulders to take my hands. He draws me with him toward the bed.

I grimace. "Amar, I—"

"You need rest."

My discomfort deepens. Rest. Right.

"What?" he asks.

I shake my head.

Amar sinks down onto the edge of the mattress, pulling me down beside him. "What?" he repeats.

"It's nothing. Stupid."

He pauses. "You say that a lot, you know."

I shift my shoulders again. He obviously doesn't understand the fine art of burying uncomfortable things.

The complete bullshit of that thought overwhelms me. But it doesn't mean I want to tell Amar I've been dreaming about him. Even if the dreams were horrible, it's still sort of embarrassing.

"Nightmares," I say.

"Ruby?"

"No, just… other stuff."

He's silent for a moment. "Do you want me to stay with you?"

I look over at him in surprise.

"For a little bit," he amends carefully. "To help you get to sleep."

I falter, taken back by how much I want to blurt out yes and how unexpected it is for him to offer anything like that where others might learn of it. My eyes skip toward the closed door. I don't suppose Bianca will find out, though. And it's not like that matters anyway. Well, sort of. Except for the part where *God* knows how she'll react if she discovers Amar has the slightest hint of feelings for me.

But then, the door's closed. And it'll only be for a short while. Maybe that's why he's suggesting it.

I nod. "Okay."

He moves to the opposite side of the bed and then slides beneath the blankets. A weird mix of exhilaration and nervousness bubbles through me as I go to join him. The silken gray sheets slip over my skin, and when I near his warmth, every little hair on my body seems to stand on end, like they're some sort of radar for my proximity to him.

But I can't stop the nervousness. This bizarre shyness just rushing through me—like despite sleeping together yesterday, I still feel oddly self-conscious around him.

Though, come to think of it, maybe what happened yesterday is why.

I look at him, only to find him watching me with the strangest expression on his face. It's almost a smile. Almost.

But I'd swear he's nervous too. The realization makes my heart race.

He shifts around, propping himself on an elbow next to me. Gently, he reaches over. His fingers brush across my jawline.

Instinctively, my eyes drift closed and my face turns toward the soothing sensation. I can't get enough of it, him touching me, even just like this. It's as if my body comes alive whenever I'm near him. Like all the horror and pain in the rest of my life fades to the background.

His hand cups my cheek. I feel him hesitate for a heartbeat, and then he draws closer. His lips brush mine.

Adrenaline overtakes my nervousness. My hand finds his side, gripping his warm skin, and my lips part. After only the briefest pause, he takes me up on the invitation. His mouth devours my own while he shifts around again, moving me back onto the sheets, moving on top of me.

It's a relief, his body on mine. It's only been a day since he was this close, but I've still missed him.

I wrap my leg around one of his, drawing him tighter against me. A pleased noise escapes him, so soft it's barely audible. I grin against his lips.

His hand slips under my nightshirt and up my side.

My breasts tingle, craving his touch, and the reward comes a moment later when his fingers embrace one of them. I turn my head to the side as Amar's lips leave mine and travel down my neck, kissing me, nipping at me, waking up every inch of me. My eyes close, my entire being relishing this sensation, and more than anything, I want him to undress me. I want to lose myself in this, to forget everything for the sheer joy of having him close to me again.

Even though I know I can't.

Amar seems to realize the same thing. He suddenly pauses in his journey down my neck, and then a breath leaves him. He's motionless for a moment before he pulls back, looking down at me in the pale moonlight.

"Rest, huh?" I tease quietly.

A smile tugs at the corner of his lip, but his eyes appear pained.

I reach up, touching the side of his face. "Later?"

The pain in his gaze lessens. He nods. "Yeah."

He kisses me briefly, and then he shifts around again to lie down at my side. Putting his arm around my shoulders, he draws me closer. I rest my head on his bare chest.

Seconds slip by.

I bite my lip. His skin feels so good beneath my cheek. His body is so comforting beside mine. But now my eyes won't stay closed. Without the distraction of his touch and taste, the whole day is coming back. Everything we've been through. What Ruby's been through.

What that troll guy said about me.

"You okay?" Amar asks softly.

I hesitate. "Who was that guy? The way he looked at you… It's like he thought he knew something about you."

A pause follows. "I've never seen him before tonight."

I try to figure out how to respond. Those words aren't quite an answer, and I think he knows it. "Amar, even those people at the set yesterday were—"

"It's nothing," he says, his voice somehow calm and yet desperate, like he doesn't want me to finish that sentence.

I don't know what to do. I could press the issue. I probably even *should*. But I'm running out of strength for this madness and all the fresh hells that seem to upend my world at every turn. I can't take much more.

"Okay," I whisper.

His hand strokes my hair, and I can't quite believe it's my imagination that some measure of tension seems to ease from him, almost like he's relieved.

It makes my stomach churn.

I force myself to close my eyes and concentrate on the gentle feeling of his hand on my hair, on the slow rise and fall of his warm chest.

And I hope like hell I'll wake up tomorrow to find this insanity has come to an end.

4

Amar's gone when I open my eyes.

I sit up and push the blankets aside. The clock on the nightstand says it's still early, and the pearlescent light streaming past the curtains seems to agree. Meanwhile, the bedroom door is closed. I can't hear anything from the hallway.

I retrieve my clothes from the chair on the far side of the room and leave my borrowed pajamas there, for lack of anything else to do. The hall is silent when I head out the door, but as I near the stairway, I pick up on Amar's voice from the floor below.

"—need to be careful."

I pause at the top of the steps. Ruby stands by the window, every line of her body tense. Amar is by her side, his attention focused on her, and it's easy to see that she's the one to whom he was speaking. She's not looking at him, though. Just like with me last night, she's not quite looking at anything.

She gives a tight nod to his words and then puts a step

of distance between them like she's trying to find somewhere else to go. Amar hesitates and then leaves her alone. He strides toward the stairs, only to stop at the sight of me.

"Good morning," he says evenly. I wonder if Bianca is anywhere nearby.

"Hey," I reply.

Ruby retreats farther into the room. I bury a grimace and start downstairs.

Amar comes to meet me.

"You told her?" I ask.

He nods, watching Ruby from the corner of his eye.

"And?"

He's silent for a moment. "We'll keep an eye on her. Make sure she's safe."

My mouth tightens, but there's nothing for it. It's not like I have a better plan. Meanwhile, Ruby's on the far side of the living room now, practically against the wall, like she's putting as much space between herself and us as possible.

It's painful to see.

"We need to get your apartment back together," Amar says quietly. "Give her somewhere familiar to go."

I glance at him, surprised by his sensitivity—although, really, I'm not sure why. He's been so kind to me every step of the way. "Yeah. Okay." I nod, even as my brain runs up against the problem of how to do that. Thanks to House Volgert, the whole place is destroyed, from the splintered furniture to the sliced mattresses. Meanwhile, I'm pretty much broke, and I doubt Ruby's up to bankrolling a remodel at the moment.

But I don't want to tell Amar that.

"Sure," I bluff. "I can—"

"I'll take care of it."

I falter, not sure how to respond. Amar shrugs.

"God, aren't you all up early?"

Bianca's voice cuts off anything I would have managed to say. I turn to see her coming down the stairs.

"We were just leaving," Amar replies, like the interruption hasn't fazed him in the least. "I'm going to make a few calls. Get Cait and Ruby's place back in order."

Bianca arches an eyebrow, her expression radiating surprise and baffled contempt.

"Unless you want them staying here from now on?" Amar continues with a wry look of his own.

There's just a heartbeat, barely noticeable, that passes before Bianca scoffs. "Whatever." Shaking her head, she walks past us and disappears into the kitchen.

"Come on," Amar says to me. "Let's get you both home."

⸺

IT TAKES ALL DAY, REPAIRING THE APARTMENT AND PICKING UP the pieces of what Volgert's people left behind. The living room is a total loss. Much of the bedrooms too. Even some of our clothes have been destroyed, ripped apart by the same assholes who'd shredded the mattresses, chairs, and couch.

Ruby never says a word, and soon I adopt silence as well. It seems better. Safer. Or maybe I don't want to confront the fact she might not respond if I spoke to her. Amar never breaks it, though. Stepping outside occasionally, he takes his cell with him and makes calls from somewhere down the hall.

And then more delivery people arrive.

Clothes come. Bedding. New mattresses, new furniture,

all of it as close as possible to what was destroyed. I catch Ruby staring at Amar from time to time like she can't figure out what to make of him, though when she realizes I've noticed her, she instantly drops her gaze away.

I never see her look at me once.

By nightfall, it's like no one ever broke in. Even the damned coffee table has been replaced, and somehow, Amar's people have succeeded in finding posters exactly identical to the ones that had been ripped from our walls. I stare around the living room, struck by how it looks more like we bought a few new things for the apartment than that we all barely survived a brush with hell over the weekend.

"Thank you," I say to Amar after the last delivery person is gone.

"Yeah," Ruby agrees. I look over. She's got her eyes on a point somewhere midway in our direction. She seems like she wants to leave.

"Of course," Amar replies.

Ruby retreats into her room and shuts her door.

An ache throbs through me. Turning away, I try to fix my attention on anything else. The tags still attached to the couch pillows, maybe. Those could be important right now.

"You okay?" Amar asks quietly.

I don't look toward him, feeling about as reluctant to meet his eyes as Ruby had appeared. "You really didn't have to do all—"

"I have the money. I'd prefer to use it for something good."

I'm not sure what to say.

"I don't suppose there's any chance of convincing you not to go tonight?" he continues.

A grimace twists my face. The salvage yard. Ram. I'd managed to forget for five seconds.

I look towards Ruby's room, guilt and anxiety gnawing at me. I don't want to leave her alone, here in this apartment, only two days after demonic bastards broke in and abducted her. I need to protect my best friend, even if I don't have a clue how to do that.

And I need to know what that troll meant. I have to know what I—what *we*—are up against.

I shake my head.

Amar sighs. "Didn't think so."

"I don't want to leave her unprotected, though. I—"

A knock comes on the door. Without a word, Amar crosses the room and answers it.

I blink at the sight of the three people standing there. I don't recognize them, but between their eerily intent gazes and their body language, their identity is clear. Werewolves, like the ones Amar and Bianca hired to help find Ruby. Silently, the trio walks past Amar, their attention on the apartment.

"Would you tell Ruby they're here?" Amar asks me. "They'll keep an eye on the place while we're gone."

I falter. He… he thought of that already. Keeping her safe. And he… "Yeah." I turn toward her bedroom, only to pause as another worry hits me. Doors aren't the only way demons get into places. "O-okay, but the shadows—"

"I've put defenses around the place too. They won't be able to get in like they did."

I can't help but stare at him this time. When did he have the chance to do that? "Thank you."

Amar shrugs a shoulder and then glances to the werewolves. "Give the girl as much space as you can, but don't let her out of your sight."

One of them nods. Amar looks back at me, his brow rising in a silent question.

I swallow hard and make myself head for Ruby's room. Silence follows my knock on the door.

"Ruby?" I inch the door open.

She's standing by her bed, running a hand over the brand-new blue comforter that looks nearly identical to the one a Volgert henchman decided to use for slicing practice.

"Ruby? I, um… I'm really sorry, but Amar and I have to go." I can't even tell if she's heard me. "There are some people here, though. They're going to help make sure nobody comes and…"

My words run out. I'm not sure what to say. Kidnaps her and nearly destroys her life again?

"What are they?"

I can barely hear her whisper. I cast a nervous glance over my shoulder and then step farther into the room. "Just people Amar hired. Like, bodyguards. They won't hurt you."

Her head turns toward me, and I can read the trace of expression on her face. She wasn't asking that. But the truth…

I brace myself. "Werewolves."

Air leaves her, shaky and rough, and she looks back toward her bed. Her fingers dig into the blue comforter.

I search for something else to say, but there's just nothing. No words to make anything make sense, no answer I can give as to why we're standing in her new-old bedroom, having a stilted conversation about things that should be confined to fantasy books. It's madness.

It feels like my fault.

"We'll be back soon," I try. "I promise. And they, um…" I cast a quick look at the door. "They won't hurt you.

They're just here to keep you safe, okay? Everything… everything's going to be safe now."

I hope.

Nothing follows my statement. Hurt swells up like a hot ball in my chest, and I want to beg her to look at me, talk to me, say *anything* just to give me somewhere to start in fixing this.

The silence feels like needles pressing into my skin.

"Okay," I manage. Nodding to nothing and no one, I retreat to the living room, fighting to get my expression and emotions under control as I go.

Amar doesn't say anything at the sight of me, only twitches his head toward the hallway. I follow him, leaving the mercenaries to find places on the new sofa and chairs.

The hall is dark around us; the landlord still hasn't repaired the wall lamp midway down the corridor. Deep pools of shadow cluster everywhere, though a square of light stretches from the window at the end of the hallway.

Amar stops at the edge of the light. I do the same, and when he extends a hand, I wrap my fingers around his warm palm without a word.

"Give her time," he says softly.

My eyes twitch up, meeting his, and I find only sympathy there.

It helps.

I take a shuddering breath, nodding at the repetition of the words he'd spoken last night. I can do that. Give her time.

I just hope that'll be enough.

5

My feet land on gravel, and the dark confines of the hallway are replaced by much more space. Blinking, I look around fast, taking in mountains of metal formed by everything from cars to washing machines to old school desks. Behind us, a security lamp blazes, its glow hitting one of the piles and creating a fine line of shadow and light on the ground behind our shoes.

And there are a thousand places for people to hide. A thousand places from which they might be watching us, ready to ambush us the moment we move.

Amar drops his hand from mine. I glance at him quickly. He's scanning the area, a sharp look in his dark eyes, but he's back to radiating calm in that way he has—like, despite our location, he's totally in control of the situation.

I envy him.

A rustle makes me jump a mile, adrenaline surging through me and making the hairs on my arms stand on end. From beyond one of the piles, Ram steps into view.

He's not alone.

Five other people emerge from the darkness around us, leaving their hiding places behind the mounds of junk, and I don't know whether they're trolls or werewolves or something else entirely. Tall and muscular, they all simply seem like they could tear us apart with their bare hands.

At the sight of Amar, the one nearest to Ram growls. Leaning over, he mutters something to the troll, who raises a hand in a calming motion.

I try not to show my alarm, but there it is again. That way people keep reacting to Amar. What the hell is—

"Hey there," Ram says to me. "Wasn't sure you'd come." His attention flicks to Amar, and he runs his eyes over him with a considering expression that grows more sardonic and resistant by the second.

And I can just read it. They're going to insist Amar leave.

"He's with me," I say into the tense silence. "He goes, I go."

Ram turns the wry look on me, but after a moment, he shrugs. "This way." He nods toward the shadowed path through the junkyard at his back.

The other guy growls again. Ram gives him an expectant glance. "Katsuro wants her here."

Anxiety prickles through me, even stronger than before. I want to leave.

I want to learn what these people know.

Glowering, the guy relents. Keeping one eye to us, he moves toward the path and Ram follows. The others step nearer to us, waiting.

Okay, then. Sticking close to Amar, I trail after Ram. The light of the security lamp falls behind us, leaving us in shadows that never seem to end. Crumpled cars are stacked one atop the other, forming blind corners that could be hiding anything. Our shoes crunching on the gravel is the only sound. My gaze skirts to the people around us; they're still watching me and Amar.

I wish I knew why the hell everyone reacts to Amar this way. I know I trust him. Even if I don't know everything about him, I've nevertheless come to trust him nearly as much as Ruby.

But still.

We round something that might have once been a school bus, and an open spread of gravel comes into view. At the heart of it, a warehouse stands. Tarps flap over what look like holes in the metal roof, and sheets of the siding hang askew. I can't see any light coming from inside.

Ram pauses by the massive metal slab of a door and glances toward the others. Without a word, the five of them head around the sides of the building, scanning the scrapyard as they go.

Despite its decrepit appearance, the door doesn't make a sound while Ram pulls it aside. Darkness envelops us when we walk into the warehouse. The air is dank with cloying humidity, and the smell of moldy hay and motor oil clings to it.

Somehow, I know we're not alone. I can't see jack shit, but I'd swear there are others in here with us. Anxious shivers make tingles run beneath my skin, like whatever I have inside wants to break out and blast everything near me into the walls.

The door closes. Before I can turn, a light flares to life.

I wasn't wrong.

Three people wait in the space up ahead. The one farthest to the right holds a green plastic camping lantern. Its blue-white LED light casts strange shadows from the hulking metal tractors on either side of us. The guy on the left has a shotgun resting against his shoulder like he's just waiting for the command to swing the weapon down and fire. And the one in the middle has nothing. His hands are clasped in front of the long, dark coat draping him, and his black hair brushes cheekbones that appear chiseled from rock. He looks Asian, maybe Japanese, and somewhere in his early thirties.

But then we walk closer and I see his eyes. They watch me, unblinking, and they send alarms ringing through me of wrong, wrong, wrong. They make him seem old. Ancient, even, like I'm looking into the eyes of someone who has seen more years go by than they could hope to count.

And I know without a doubt that he's the one in charge and *absolutely* the most dangerous of the three.

The tingling in my skin gets worse. I make myself keep breathing while I silently beg the magic inside me to stay under control.

"Cait," Ram says, gesturing to me and then glancing to the Asian guy.

The man steps forward, extending a hand. "Welcome." His voice is smooth. Polished. It reminds me of a river stone. "My name is Hisakawa Katsuro. A pleasure to meet you."

Nervously, I take his hand.

It's inhumanly cool. My breath catches.

His smile returns, stronger this time. "Apologies. You haven't shaken hands with a vampire before, I take it."

My heart starts pounding harder. "No."

His brow shrugs impartially at my answer. "It can be alarming. I should have warned you." He glances at Amar. "Hello to you as well, Mister Okoro."

Amar gives him a slight nod in response, and his eyes track the man when Katsuro steps back from me again. "You wanted Cait here," Amar says. "She's here. Now what is this about?"

Ram's lip twitches. He looks at the vampire.

"We would like Cait's help," Katsuro replies.

I tense, the words so close to what Kyle had said after he took Ruby.

"With what?" Amar presses.

Katsuro glances at me. "You would be safer having this conversation if this gentleman was not present, you know."

I shiver. I have no idea what he's talking about, but right now, I don't care. I'll ask Amar later.

Assuming we make it out of here.

I shove the thought aside. "Amar stays. Answer the question."

Amusement flickers over Katsuro's face. "Very well. How much do you know about what House Linden and House Volgert are currently fighting over?"

My brow twitches down warily. "Not... not a lot."

He nods like he'd expected the response. "And how much do you know about the Touched?"

My shivering grows stronger. Colder, like it's commencing an assault on my core.

God, don't let this have anything to do with Ruby...

"Some," I manage.

He nods a second time, though he glances over briefly like he's taking note of whatever he sees on Amar's face. My eyes dart Amar's way. Stone again. He has that non-expression down to a science.

I can't tell what Katsuro thinks of it, though. "The insanity," the vampire continues to me. "Like what I assume happened to your friend, considering her location last night?"

I'm not sure what to say. What other part is there? "Yeah…"

He looks at Amar again. "Have you heard of the rest of it?"

I follow his gaze. He isn't taking his eyes from Amar this time, like Katsuro is judging his reaction to the words.

"What 'rest of it'?" I ask.

A heartbeat passes before Katsuro returns his attention to me. "You are not like the others, are you? The succubi and incubi. You care about humans and innocents. People other than yourself."

Confusion hits me. This isn't an answer to my question. "Uh, yeah? I mean, I guess—"

"And if you could do something to assist the Touched… would you?"

My confusion grows. "Of course."

His smile returns. It sends anxiety crawling down my spine.

"What is this about?" Amar demands.

Katsuro seems to weigh his words as he clasps his hands behind his back. "Approximately twenty-five years ago, the Houses made a discovery. The subtle magical energy that flows through our world—the magic demons instinctively draw upon and direct so freely in numerous aspects of our lives—is changing. Now, the details behind this are complex, and many of the potential ramifications are as well, but one result is now undeniable." He gives a humorless smile. "*Humans* have been affected. They have been changed by magic, yet they have no idea that it has happened and—barring a few catalyzing factors brought about by incubi or succubi—they show no sign of that change at all."

"That's impossible," Amar says.

"Oh, I'm aware of the common knowledge. We all are." Katsuro skims his eyes over the others around him. "Demons have existed easily as long as humanity and quite possibly longer. If humanity was going to experience any effects from their proximity to magical energy, surely we would have seen evidence of that fact prior to now. But that assumes a static system, which magic most certainly is not. A massive system, yes, but not static. And consider this: even on the smaller scale of our own influence, things have hardly stayed the same. Until a few centuries ago, the majority of demonkind stayed away from humans. We fed on them, yes, but otherwise, we lived in forests. On mountains. This is how there came to be stories of monsters in woodlands and caves. But then the world got smaller. Remote places stopped being so remote, and there weren't many—if any—places to hide from human notice any longer."

He gestures to the lantern and the tractors around us. "It's all a product of the Industrial Age. The Technology Age. We had no choice but to join the human race and blend as best we could. For some like you and I, who *naturally* look like them, it is easier. For others such as trolls, not as much. But the point is that for the first time in history, demons were not merely visiting human spaces and exposing them to our abilities for short periods. Our use of magic has now permeated all parts of the world in a way never before seen. Magical beings can be living in the apartment across the hall. Sitting in the next office cubicle. Ringing up your groceries at the store. There is no delineation of human and demonic areas any longer. Add that to the overall shifts in the magical energy of this world and you have a situation which was bound to have consequences."

"But what does that have to do with the incubi and succubi?" Amar asks.

"Plenty." Katsuro chuckles. I'm reminded of a lecturer —one who knows more than I could imagine. "Throughout history, there have been copious examples to support the idea that when certain kinds of demons direct their magic at humans, they alter them. A vampire, for instance, can feed their blood to a human and make more of our kind. Succubi and incubi can drive a human mad, creating the Touched. But recently, the Houses discovered something new. Certain humans, *rare* humans, were being transformed in different ways. And when your kind turned them into Touched..." Katsuro's brow rises and falls illustratively, "these hidden ones became something else entirely."

I stare at him. "Like what?"

"Touched... with special abilities. Not the same as *your* kind—not exactly. They only manifest talents like you, not the innate skills that make you what you are."

His words don't make any sense to me. Hell, none of this does.

Katsuro seems to see my confusion. He glances at Amar like he's checking something, and whatever he sees brings that dark amusement back into his eyes. "I take it your friend hasn't mentioned that."

Amar is silent, but it feels like the temperature in the room plummets.

Katsuro doesn't appear to care. "Succubi and incubi are among the most magically versatile of all demons," he explains to me. "Perhaps it's a product of evolution; you deal in seduction, not direct violence, and thus, your prey requires more finesse to hunt than, say, a vampire or werewolf might need. And certainly, there are several other species who've come close to you in this regard, maybe even one or two members among the remaining species who will manifest special skills in the way many of you do... but no other demonic type does it as consistently."

"I—" My eyes twitch to Amar. "I don't understand."

"Think of it like this," Katsuro says. "Humans have talents, correct? Inherent abilities that exceed their fellow humans in certain ways, occasionally to an almost unbelievable degree. And some demons—your kind especially—have similar. But *unlike* an ordinary human, your talents are magical. Supernatural. Extraordinary. And when the specific humans who have been affected by the shift in the magical energy of this world are turned into Touched, they too manifest these supernatural skills." His expression turns pointed. "But the problem, of course, is that those humans are still insane. They are still rabid and desperate and crave being fed like any of the Touched. And yet they have these talents, turning them effectively into *you*, but without the pesky inconvenience of possessing free will."

The shivers return, scurrying over my skin.

Katsuro glances at Amar again. "Even a demon who's sworn to a House can leave. Not that they do very *often*—" His tone becomes biting. "—owing to the fact *most* of them would spend the rest of their lives hiding in terror, since their former House would readily make an example of them for the offense. But it happens. They can refuse an order. They can be unpredictable. But a Touched?" Katsuro gestures evenly. "They are the perfect slave."

I feel sick.

"That is whom Linden and Volgert are fighting over. A

Touched—or perhaps simply the rumor of one—freshly turned from human only a short time ago. The story is that this newly made Touched has manifested an incredible ability, one that even the succubi and incubi haven't possessed in centuries, though the rumors are vague as to what that might be. But Volgert wants them. They seem to think Linden controls them, though if they do, Linden is keeping them well hidden. In the meantime, though, Volgert is tearing into the Linden Protected, sending the message that Linden cannot defend their own, so they ought to capitulate to Volgert's demands. Thus far, Linden has shown no intention of doing so. Once Volgert realizes this fact, they will escalate their aggression, and then *all* of us will be looking at a war."

I can't stop shaking. I don't even know what that means—a war—but I know it can't be good. For me. For Amar. Ruby. Anyone I've met.

The Houses have been terrifying enough, and they've hardly even started *fighting* yet.

"How do you fit into all this?" Amar's voice doesn't reveal a hint of what he thinks of Katsuro's words, but suddenly, I remember he said something about this. Ages ago—or, you know, last week—when he first took me to Bianca's apartment... Amar had been concerned about the Houses starting a war too.

At his question now, though, one of the guys beside Katsuro gives a low growl. Katsuro glances at him. "Then we will know who to blame."

The other guy appears slightly mollified. I look between them, not liking the sound of that.

"The answer to your question is complicated," Katsuro continues, directing the words at Amar. "*Very.* And quite frankly, I am not certain we can trust you." His gaze flicks to me briefly, considering. "Suffice it to say that we are the counterbalance to this. We are the force which will stop it."

"Stop what?" I ask nervously. "The war?"

"All of it. The Touched. The sets. The ones being used for the powers they manifest. The Houses and their myriad ways of exploiting humanity and meddling in this world. Everything."

I stare at him.

"Suicide," Amar states.

Ram shifts angrily. "Guts."

"We know the risks in undermining the system the Houses have built," Katsuro says. "Why do you think we've been so careful about meeting with her?" He nods at me. "Why do you think there are guards outside right now, if not to protect against the possibility that any one of us were followed? We are well aware of the danger and of what the Houses do to the people who oppose them."

"I doubt that."

My stomach churns at the darkness lurking in Amar's voice.

One of the guys near us growls like a wolf, his eyes flashing bright like backlit amber. He starts forward as if he's going to attack, but Ram's hand comes up fast, catching the man's chest to stop him.

Katsuro doesn't even glance their way. "Your opinion is irrelevant. We are not like others of our kind, and we are *certainly* not like your type. The demon-born among us aren't willing to pretend they are a superior race to the humans, and the changed in our number—the vampires or werewolves—haven't forgotten what it was to be human ourselves. We feed on them, yes. But we can choose *not* to kill. And we know that if not for being turned, it could have been *us* in those pits. It could be *our* friends and family devoured by this sick system of death matches and exploitation. What the Houses have done to these people is wrong. It's an offense any decent person should do whatever they can to stop."

The air gets colder. Arctic in its bite.

And there's something in Katsuro's voice, a knife's edge of fury sliding under his placid tone. It sounds like this is personal. It makes my heart race. "How are you going to help them?" I ask before Amar can speak.

For an eternal moment, my question is met with silence. Finally, Katsuro looks away from Amar, but he still hesitates before answering me. "That is part of why we need your assistance. It's uncommon enough to save a Touched person from their madness, and these humans who've manifested abilities like your kind…" He grimaces slightly. "It may be difficult to bring them back to sanity again. Matters are made more complex by the fact that it takes a succubus or incubus to dismantle what was done to them, and—as you may have noticed—your kind are rather lacking in the compassion department. They would never aid a Touched without an egregiously self-serving motive. You are the only one who is different. The only one I've met in centuries who—if you will forgive what is an offensive comparison to the rest of your kind—is still human inside. This makes you invaluable to us and to our cause."

I'm not sure what to say. He's never quite looked at Amar, but I think we're nearing deep space for a temperature in here.

I fight the urge to fidget with discomfort. Everything else aside, this could be bullshit. Katsuro could simply want to get his hands on these people for himself. There's no reason to assume he isn't lying.

But if he *is* telling the truth…

"What's the other part of why you want my help?" I ask.

"We want you to find them for us."

I stare at him, flabbergasted.

"No," Amar replies immediately.

Ram gives him a disgusted look. "Not your call, incubus."

"Cait is the one the Houses will come after," Katsuro says. "It is her life at risk, regardless of whether she helps us, and for the very reason I've already mentioned. Her talent. The one that, now that I've seen her, I am certain she stands a good chance of possessing. The Houses have only resisted carving a trail of blood through whole cities and changing all in their path to Touched because of the dangerous human attention it would draw. Yet, depending upon the form her talent takes, Cait might be able to help them find those rare few they need—and even if she cannot, they won't leave the possibility unexplored. They *will* come for her. But we can help. We can protect her. And we can give her the opportunity to do something good with her heritage."

"What are you talking about?" I ask. "What heritage?"

"Josephine," Katsuro says. "Your mother."

My world goes still.

"You are the very image of her, you are the right age to be her child, and it appears your demonic parent never arrived to claim you. These facts point squarely to Josephine being your mother, something which cannot have escaped the Houses' attention. You won't remain free of them much longer without help."

I can't speak. I don't have a clue what Katsuro *means*,

but I can't even speak. I look toward Amar, desperate for a lifeline.

He's totally frozen. I'm not even sure he's breathing. But there's something to his stillness, like he understands exactly who they're talking about.

And it's shocked the hell out of him.

"But—" I begin.

A loud noise cuts me off. On instinct, I look at the door like I can see through to the outside. Shouting breaks out, and then the sound of gunfire too.

"Go!" Ram orders.

I turn. The man with the lantern bends quickly and yanks open a hatch I hadn't noticed in the floor. Ram and the others hurry toward it.

"This way!" Katsuro calls, motioning for me to follow.

Something heavy slams into the door. Metal screeches in protest, and a crash follows the sound.

Electricity burns the air behind me. I can feel it coming, the incredible heat building in the time it takes to blink. I don't have time to react.

Amar grabs me. Shoves me forward, past the line of shadow cast by the lantern and the tractors.

Darkness swallows me.

6

I tumble onto grass. A weight slams into my back, smashing the air from my chest.

And then the world explodes.

Frantically, I cover my head. Debris scatters over me, and I cringe under the assault. I can't hear. My ears ring from the blast of whatever the hell was just destroyed.

The bombardment ends almost as quickly as it began, and the weight on me disappears. My lungs labor hard to draw in air while sound comes to me thick and muffled like my head is wrapped in cotton. Someone is shouting. I can't make sense of the words.

Choking with my effort to breathe, I roll over, searching for Amar.

I find him. He's surrounded. Six guys with knives circle him. We're in the middle of a park not far from my apartment, and up ahead, a tree looks like it's been hit with a grenade. Orange flames climb from the shattered trunk. Smoke blurs the streetlights, casting cold light on the grass.

I rush to my feet, woodchips falling from my clothes and skin. "Amar!"

Two of the guys feint toward him. They slash at him with their knives like they want to tear him apart. I can't see any magic on Amar yet, no blue glow or faint crackle of electricity, but when he twitches back, the ones nearest to him pull away, as if even with their knives, they're scared of getting too close.

"Cait, run!" he shouts.

I don't move. I'm not leaving him here. "Get the hell away from him!"

No one listens. The ones around Amar don't even blink.

But two of them break off from the group and charge toward me.

I retreat on the slick grass. A strange sensation pulses through me, like all the air around me rushes toward my body and then bursts away.

I remember the feeling. It's what happened in the alley outside Goa Café.

The men stagger. One of them falls, but the second lunges at me. His hands grab my arms. His weight tears me down. I tumble to the ground, and he comes with me.

My fingers claw at the grass while I struggle to drag myself away. He reaches out quickly, snagging my shirt. His other hand grabs my shoulder and hauls me back to the dirt and grass.

"Stay still, bitch." He places his knife to my neck. "You're no good to the Guardians in pieces."

I don't listen. On instinct, a tangle of purple energy washes over me, masking the world in fog for all of a heartbeat. The guy cries out. His grip and the knife disappear. I scramble to my feet, my body feeling electrified.

I don't make it far. Hands catch me again. Shove me to the grass and then yank me around.

The first guy I knocked down glares at me. "You'll pay for that." His knife flashes in the darkness. His other hand wraps around my neck.

Panic races through my body. My fingers pry at his own while my eyes lock on the blade hovering above me. White sparks flare across the shadows encroaching on my vision. A rushing sound fills my ears, made up of too much blood with no way to escape.

And I can't breathe. I just can't breathe. The blade starts toward me.

A surge of energy rushes by me, tingling and weirdly cold, and every hair on my body stands on end. I hear a muffled shout, and his grip vanishes. I gag, my hands clutching my burning throat. My whole body feels like alarm bells are clanging throughout my system, each one ringing with panic from the fact I almost died.

Someone grabs my shoulder. I shriek, my legs and hands already fighting to get me away.

"Cait!"

My eyes focus. Amar is there. Relief hits me like a two-by-four, making me want to sob.

Hanging onto him for support, I scramble up from the grass and throw a panicked glance at the park. Our attackers are on the ground.

All of them.

I look at Amar, incredulous.

His mouth tightens. "Let's go." He heads for the street.

Anxiously, I jog after him. We cross the road, leaving the park behind, and duck into an alleyway between two businesses that have already closed for the night.

The moment we reach the alley, Amar moves me

behind him. Keeping us both in the shadows, he scans the street and the park. I peer past him, but there's nothing. Nobody but those guys on the ground, still not moving. I don't know what he did to them. How he managed to take out six—

My eyes play a trick on me, and suddenly, two women and three more guys materialize out of the shadows near the trees. And my brain can't keep up. It's as if they were there the whole time. Like my mind is arguing that surely I only missed them, but I know it's not true.

Their eyes sweep the park, pausing briefly on the destroyed tree and then landing on the fallen guys. Amar pushes me farther behind him, his attention never leaving the group. In the distance, I hear sirens. Police, maybe, or firemen responding to the reports of an explosion. They're coming closer with every second.

One of the women motions to the others, and together, they head toward the men on the ground. They heft the guys between them and carry them across the grass till they reach a point where the glow of a streetlight casts a shadow from a tree.

And the world shifts again. The group is gone.

Amar lets out a small breath.

I draw in air of my own, realizing I haven't breathed since the five people appeared. Amar glances back at me, and I catch how his gaze pauses at my throat.

I swallow. The motion hurts, and I try not to think what bruises might show up there by tomorrow. As if I didn't have enough things to figure out how to explain to Ruby…

I shove the thought aside. Hard.

"Come on," Amar says. "We need to get out of here."

He heads deeper into the alleyway. Casting an anxious glance over my shoulder, I follow. The alley empties onto a narrow side street. The shadows are thicker, with almost no light to interrupt them. Somehow, that almost seems comforting.

"Who were those people?" I whisper to him. "Who are the Guardians?"

He slams to a halt. I stop fast, barely keeping myself from bumping into him.

"*What?*"

"The Guardians," I repeat. "The guy said I was no good to them if I was dead." My words are met with silence. "Amar? Who are they?"

"Revolutionaries. Psychotic ones."

My brow climbs. Oh, fantastic. There are those too now? "Any idea why they'd attack Katsuro's people?"

He doesn't respond for a moment. "We need to get moving. Get back to your place."

I guess that's a no. At least… possibly.

He starts off again, and I don't think it's my imagination that he looks even more tense than before.

My stomach lodged firmly into a knot, I hurry after him.

⤬

By the time we step out of the shadows across the street from my apartment, my heart feels like a drum pounding loud enough to wake the world. For several moments, Amar keeps us out of sight behind the corner of a building across the street, watching for who knows what, before we rush toward the entrance and inside.

I shut the door behind us, wishing it had more than just a simple lock. My arms and legs tingle with adrenaline and the feeling like I'm a rabbit barely escaping a trap. But no one pounds on the door. No demons step from the shadows. I swallow down a harried breath and turn away from the entrance, trying desperately to calm myself down.

And then I hesitate with alarm, the stairwell light letting me see clearly for the first time. Bits of wood are snarled in the fabric of Amar's shirt, and he has scratches all over his neck and arms. He starts up the steps without a word, but from the stinging of my own skin, I can guess my injuries probably look the same. I bite my lip and trail after him, grateful we weren't closer to whatever hit that tree.

My place is silent when we slip inside. On the couch and chairs, the mercenaries sit, their eyes locked on us. I get the weird impression they'd known we were coming.

They rise from the seats. One of them twitches his head back toward Ruby's door. "She hasn't left."

Amar nods. "Keep watch outside. We were followed from the meeting. I blocked our path of shadow-crossing, but they may still try to track us here."

The werewolves nod in return, though their eyes flick over us like they've read something between the lines. In silence, the group files from the apartment.

And then it's just me and Amar.

"Do you have any bandages?" he asks softly.

"Y-yeah, of course." I hurry toward the bathroom. Several seconds of digging turns up a box of Band-Aids and some antibiotic ointment that doesn't expire for another month. I gather them quickly and bring them back to the living room. "Do you want me to get you a wash-cloth or—"

I cut off, seeing he's already gathered some paper towels and a small cup of water. He glances at Ruby's bedroom and then nods toward mine. I slip past him and wait to close the door until after he's inside.

He sits on the edge of the bed and sets the cup of water and the paper towels on the nightstand next to him. Not quite looking his way, I sink down near him.

"Let me see that," he says, taking my arm gently.

"What about you?"

"In a minute."

He dips the edge of a paper towel into the cup and then starts cleaning the tiny traces of dried blood from my cuts. His motions are so tender, so careful, as he works his way up my arm to the scrapes on my cheek. I watch him, though he never meets my eyes. Every few moments, a flicker of worry crosses his face, and there's something strange in the expression, as if the sight of the small wounds isn't the only thing upsetting him.

I wonder if it's the same thing that's bothering me.

"You, uh…" I'm not sure how to ask. "You recognized who Katsuro was talking about. Josephine."

He's silent. It doesn't matter. I know what I saw at the salvage yard.

"Who is she?"

He sets the wet paper towel aside and takes up a dry one. Carefully, he pats the moisture from my arms and cheek.

"Amar?"

"I never met her," he admits, not looking away from what he's doing. "I only heard of her."

I wait, barely breathing.

He returns the paper towel to the nightstand and then picks up the antibiotic ointment. "She worked for Volgert."

I hesitate at the short statement. Worked. Past tense. "What did she do?"

He's silent while he finishes with the ointment. Never meeting my eyes, he retrieves the box of Band-Aids. "She read things about people."

My brow furrows when nothing else follows. "Read things?"

Amar places a bandage on the largest of the slices on my arm and then reaches over for another Band-Aid. I put a hand on his, stopping him. Most of the cuts are so tiny, there's no point in covering them. And I want to hear what he knows.

"Like what?" I prompt anxiously.

"She saw if they were lying. If they weren't who they claimed to be."

"So they think I can do that too," I fill in, barely asking. "Read people."

He nods.

"Well, but—" I search for words. "What's so special about—"

"Houses use spies, Cait." He looks up for the first time. "They spy on each other constantly. Add to that conspiracies *within* the Houses—and the fact that when spies aren't good enough, assassins are there to fill the void—and you've got a whole slew of dangerous people who aren't what they seem. Someone like Josephine, someone like *you*, who could spot those people at a glance…" He shakes his head. "You'd be the first line of defense against all of that, and about the best one any House could have."

I exhale sharply, looking away. Kyle. I hadn't liked him. Alistair. I'd been suspicious of him from the start too.

Amar and how I knew, just *knew*, he was trustworthy.

But that could be chalked up to anything. Lots of people have good instincts. Just because I happen to have been right about—

Amar shifts his hand around, wrapping mine with his own, and I realize I've started shaking. I don't want to be this. A target of the Houses, Katsuro's people, and who knows who else.

Even more of a freak.

"So what happened?" I ask, my voice small. "She doesn't work for Volgert anymore?"

He's silent for a few moments. "There was a power struggle between several of the Houses. I never heard what it was about—just another fight—but near the end of it, she was sent on a mission, and she—" He hesitates. "She was killed. Most likely to keep Volgert from continuing to use her abilities."

I tremble harder. Drawing in a rough breath, I reach over and grab a paper towel. I dip it in the water quickly and then turn back to him, avoiding his eyes.

"Cait," Amar starts gently.

"So that's why she never found me, huh?" I wipe the blood from his arm. "Why she didn't try to take me—"

His hand comes to rest on mine, stilling my cleaning, and I'm not even sure what I'm upset about. I never knew her. What difference does it make if she's dead? Especially since, while my stepmother, Arlene, was terrible, a demonic parent would absolutely have been worse. Amar's asshole father was proof of that.

And Josephine would have taken me away from Dad. The mere thought makes me nauseated.

So why does this hurt so much?

Amar's hand rises, brushing my cheek, the motion tender and kind. "Yeah," he answers.

My chest aches. "But what if she, I don't know, escaped and forgot or didn't—"

"It's kind of a rule among the demons, finding any

Legacy offspring you might have. Shielding the demonic world from humans is about the only thing demons agree on. Some have it easier. Vampires, werewolves… they can't have kids with humans. But succubi and incubi can, and it's a big risk. If a Legacy was discovered by humans and it came out that the demonic parent hadn't tried to find them first…" He shakes his head. "Even Volgert wouldn't protect her from that. She would have come for you if she were still alive."

My skin crawls at the image of Arlene or my stepsisters discovering what I was. And as for my dad… if he'd had to learn I wasn't even fully *human*…

"Has that ever happened?" I ask hoarsely. "One of them not, you know…"

Amar hesitates. "It's rare." At my expression, he grimaces. "There was a kid a few years ago. An incubus, about fifteen. His father never got around to finding him, but this fringe religious group out in New Mexico did. Thought he was some kind of angel. It got fairly messy before the Houses intervened."

"What'd they do?"

He's quiet for a long time. "The group died in a fire. Kid did too. The father… his House made sure no one would find all the pieces."

I feel sick all over again.

"You're lucky," he says quietly. "I don't know how you've managed not to show any sign of what you are till now, but I'm glad you didn't."

I shiver. Lucky. Right.

I wonder if the Houses would have killed my dad.

My nausea grows stronger.

Amar puts an arm around me. A rough breath shudders from my chest. I lean against him, closing my eyes and losing myself for a moment in the feeling of his comfort. In the compassion he hides from the world so much of the time.

"Do you think Katsuro was telling the truth?" I ask. "These Touched? What Linden and Volgert are fighting over?"

I feel him shake his head. "I don't know."

I nod. I don't either. And right now, it feels so much like a distant second to finding out about my mother.

About this bizarre skill I might possess.

"You don't have to do anything you don't want to," Amar says quietly. "Join them, join a House, any of it. You can stay out of it."

I shift around to look at him, a thought striking me. "How did you do it?"

My question feels a bit desperate, and the way my heart pounds only adds to the feeling. Amar hesitates, though, and I can see it: the beginnings of that closed-off look. The way he wants to shut something away inside himself. "Amar…"

"I made a deal," he says like he's forcing himself to speak the words instead of hiding.

I wait, not breathing.

"I promised the leader of Volgert that I wouldn't get involved with the Houses or their concerns."

I stare at him. "But—" I exhale, flabbergasted by the obvious. "You're helping me."

He pauses. "Yeah."

I don't know what to say. "Why?"

Amar shifts uncomfortably, like he'd rather escape the question.

I start to open my mouth to push him for an answer, and then another thought occurs to me. "Who'd you promise?" I wrack my brain for the name I remember hearing. "Lucretia?"

The discomfort in his expression strengthens. "Lucretia Volgert. Yeah."

That explains who she is, then. But as for *everything* else…

"And that was all it took?" I prompt. "Just promising her you wouldn't get involved?"

He's silent.

"So if I—"

He looks away.

"Amar?"

"Lucretia was my father's… employer. She made an exception for me."

He chooses the term carefully, I can tell. It makes my skin crawl, and I don't even know why. For what his father was, maybe. For the kind of person who would hire him, or for Amar being forced to make a deal with this woman for his freedom.

For how much history I can hear in the words.

Amar lets out a breath. "There'll be a way to keep you out of this too. You won't need to make any deals or throw in with Katsuro, his people, or anybody else. You *will* be able to stay out of things in this world."

He says the words firmly, too firmly, and he never meets my eyes. I can't help but think he's trying to convince himself as much as me. Like, maybe he's not so sure anymore. After all, I may have an ability that got my birth mother killed, and helping me has tangled him up in more trouble than he has probably seen in years.

At this point, staying out of anything might take a miracle.

I look down, not sure what to feel. I wish I hadn't

messed anything up for him—messed it up more than I'd even realized. I wish there *was* a way out of this.

I just can't see it.

Amar's hand comes up, gently brushing a strand of hair from my face, and in spite of everything, tension leaks from me at the soothing sensation.

"It's going to be okay," he assures me softly, and a bit desperately.

I nod, wanting to believe the words.

His fingers slip toward my shoulders and tease along the edge of my shirt at my neck. My skin seems to wake up at the contact, little shivers tingling through me like silent pleas for him to continue.

Silent pleas for him to give me anything else to think about right now.

I turn to him. Amar is watching me, and at the look in his eyes, the shivers grow stronger, warmer, like heat is spreading from his touch down to my core. My own gaze drops almost in desperation to escape it, but my focus only lands on his incredible lips and stops there, trapped.

He comes closer. His lips brush mine once, twice, and then they part and nip at my own, urging me to open to him. I do, needing his heat, his taste. His mouth moves with mine while his hands slip down to the bottom of my shirt, slip beneath it. A short breath leaves me at the feeling of his fingertips against my skin.

Gently, he pulls my shirt up. I break from him, frustration twisting through me at being forced to stop kissing him, but I also want him to touch more of me. I lift my arms. The fabric blocks my view of him for the moment it takes him to draw the material over my head. He drops it to the carpet. My skin prickles at the cool touch of the air.

His gaze roams over me, over my breasts still held in

the pale satin of my bra, before returning to my eyes. There's a desperate look to him. A hunger to make this better that matches my own. He moves toward me again.

But I want something to look at too.

I reach out, stopping him with my hands on his shirt. I take the hem and draw the fabric up quickly. He helps, shrugging out of it and then letting it fall.

That's better.

My hand slips around his side while he comes toward me again, his mouth claiming mine and his tongue tangling with my own. I can feel the sweat drying on his back, the bits of wood that made their way past his shirt to stick to his skin, and I know I'm sweaty too. He doesn't seem to care, though. I know I don't. He's shifting around now, his lips never leaving mine, and I scoot back on the bed, hungry to feel more of him on me.

Because we're going to be all right. We'll figure this out.

We have so far.

His fingers rake up through my hair, supporting me while I lie back on the bed and gripping me at the same time. The fabric of my comforter scrapes at the bruises and cuts on my back, but the pain only lasts a moment. He grabs the edge of the bedspread, yanking it down. I shift around, bracing myself briefly, and then the cool sheets are beneath me, Amar is above me, and I forget about the blankets entirely.

God, I missed this.

I arch my spine, giving him access to my bra clasp, and he takes me up on the offer immediately. The hooks give, the elastic loosening. He tugs the thing from me. I hear it rustle when it hits the nightstand. His lips take my breast. His hand cups one while his mouth devours the other, and my heart is pounding so hard I'm sure he can hear it. I run my hands over his shoulders, pulling at him, feeling his weight between my legs pressing deliciously on me.

I want more.

A breathless sound escapes me, and my attention skates toward the closed door, the thin walls. We have to be quiet, *so* quiet. Ruby could hear if we're too loud.

The wolves could hear.

But then, Amar sent them away.

I reach for his jeans. He lifts himself, supporting himself on one elbow, and he takes something from his pocket. His wallet. I don't know why. But he sets it behind him, not looking away from me, and nods toward his pants, an almost hopeful look in his dark, confident eyes.

My fingers open the clasp, but I don't have the leverage I need. I shift around quickly, slipping from beneath him and returning to the bottom of the bed. He rolls over and lifts himself again, giving me space while I pull his jeans away.

I glance up again when I finish. He's watching me. I can see his chest rising and falling, his breaths faster than normal.

A smile plays across my lips. I kick his pants aside and start to take off my own. His eyes never leave me, tracing my breasts, my hips, my curves while I slip the jeans down and then step from the rumpled pile of denim on the floor.

It's thrilling.

I climb back onto the bed. He pushes away from the mattress with one arm and reaches for me with the other, drawing me toward him on my hands and knees, and kissing me the moment I come close. His hand moves between us, teasing at the edge of my underwear before slipping beneath it.

I can't keep from moaning against his lips when his

fingers part the soft flesh between my legs and start massaging me there. Oh God, I want him inside me now.

With one hand, I reach back, struggling not to take my mouth from his, and I tug my underwear away. It falls to my knees, and it's awkward, getting it off from there, but I manage. Kicking it off my heel, I pay no attention to where it lands.

Amar's hand doesn't stop. It's intolerable. I rock my hips toward him, begging him for mercy, for more than this, with short noises that I fight to keep quiet. But it doesn't matter; the small motions continue unchanged, torturing me more and more with every second.

Okay, then.

Bracing myself on the soft mattress, I slide my free hand beneath his briefs and grasp his cock.

My heart pounds harder. I haven't touched him there before, not like this. But I love the feel of him. Strong, warm, soft but hard like iron under silk. It's incredible. I run my hand along his shaft, teasing at the tip of him, wondering what I can do to make him go as crazy as he's making me.

I don't have long to question. His lips break from me with a soft gasp, and then his grip shifts. He takes my shoulders, moving me back. His eyes meet mine for a moment, and I can see him breathing hard.

I smile.

It seems all the invitation he needs. He looks away, one hand going for his wallet and flipping it open fast. He tugs a condom from inside.

Ah. Finally.

Releasing me briefly, he extracts his legs from mine and pulls his briefs away. They join my clothes on the floor.

Quickly, he rips the small wrapper open and rolls the condom on.

His eyes find mine again.

Anticipation and nervousness thrum through me, but I climb over him anyway. His hand finds my ass, drawing me closer, guiding me down. I'm already so wet for him, and for one moment, the tip of him slips against me, seeking purchase, seeking entrance.

And then his cock pushes inside me.

I exhale, trying to relax and let him into me. It's like I can feel every inch of him, every centimeter sliding in, and I've missed this. *God*, I've missed this. Gently, I ease onto his hips and rock against him while I test the sensation of having him from this angle. It's different. Firmer inside me.

I like it.

A grin tugs at my lip. I press down on him, taking him in deeper, wanting all of him I can have. Amar grips me and pulls me against him, a satisfied noise leaving him. One hand releases me only to return to my clit and rub me there.

Fuck yes.

I rock against him harder, riding him, and I clamp my lips shut to hold in a moan. I don't want to wake Ruby. And the wolves, I don't know if they're back.

But oh God…

I drive myself against him harder, over and over, feeling him hitting me so deep inside. My breaths start to become shallow gasps, and it's so difficult to stop myself from making a sound. I want to let him know how good this feels. How good *he* feels.

My eyes find his, and he's watching me like he's drinking this in. Like he's enjoying every bit of what he's doing to me. I try for a smile, but everything feels so amazing that it turns into a grimace that has nothing to do with pain.

He smiles in return. His hand shifts its motion on my clit, finding some part of me that's impossibly even more sensitive, and my eyes fly wide. A gasp escapes me. His grip tightens on my hip in response, stopping me from moving away.

But God... oh my *God*...

My mouth opens. I can't even breathe. He's hitting me so deep, so hard, and every impact seems to melt my muscles. Heat and wetness is building up between us, and it's everything I can do to keep moving on him. Rocking on him. Thrusting him as deep within me as I can possibly, *possibly*—

I choke on a cry. My body collapses against his while the white heat of orgasm erupts in me and floods my veins. I lose the bed. The room. My mind feels catapulted straight into oblivion, bright and scattershot with bliss. Short, begging sounds leave me, muffled in my pillows, held back desperately because I can't wake Ruby. Can't let the wolves...

He thrusts against me harder, rough breaths leaving him. His hands grab me, pulling me down on his cock and grinding my clit against him. It's so difficult not to scream. My fingers dig into the bed. I clutch the sheets in my fist, hanging on, fighting not to cry out with how much I'm loving this.

Another orgasm builds in me, tingling through my veins before rising like a tidal wave, poised to crash over me and swallow me whole. His hands grasp me so tight, driving me onto him, relentless. I can hear him gasping with effort, with need. His scent fills my head, spice and heat and something I can only identify as *him*, all of it as intoxicating as an aphrodisiac. I inhale it while my fingers find his side, his ass against the sheets, and clutch him as tightly as I can. My weight is supported by his. My body rides his, at the mercy of his own yet safely in his control while he thrusts into me harder and harder. I could have this forever, do this forever with him, if only he wouldn't stop—

The wave of orgasm takes me, carrying my thoughts away, and I hang onto only enough awareness of the world to know I can't make a sound. Don't want to make a sound. And I don't want this to end either. I'm lost in something stronger, different than before. My entire body seems to disappear for an eternal moment. I become air. Become atoms, each one comprised of euphoria.

My body reassembles itself, coming back to the sensation of my sensitive breasts slipping against him, to my skin wet with the sweat that's broken out over my body. I feel Amar grasp me tight, clutching my head, my back, and drawing me against him like he's hanging onto me for dear life too. Huffs of desperation leave him. His thrusting accelerates. I rock onto him as hard as I can, giving him whatever I have and hoping this is good for him too.

A quiet groan leaves him, choked like it would be so much louder if not for where we are.

"Cait," he breathes. "Oh God, Cait…"

Joy bubbles up in me at the sound of my name, at the sound of his desire. His fingers dig into my skin. His thrusting becomes more deliberate, like he's driving the last of himself into me, and he's breathing so hard, it's like he ran a marathon.

With a final gasp, his thrusts begin to slow. His body relaxes, as does mine. I can feel my heart pounding in my chest, my throat, and I don't have a hope of slowing it down. Beneath me, his breaths are ragged, and for a moment, he simply lies there like he's getting his bearings.

My fingers release their death grip on the sheets. My body shakes when I push up from the bed to support myself on one elbow.

Amar looks up at me. A smile teases at his lips.

I smile too. "Whoa," I whisper.

His smile widens. "Whoa," he agrees softly.

A blush burns up my already flushed cheeks. I drop my gaze. My God, and I thought *last* time was good…

Biting my lip, I ease away from him, feeling him slip from inside me. I scoot down on the sheets, the fabric clinging to my sweaty skin, while he removes the condom and drops it into the small trash can that's crammed in the corner between my desk and my nightstand.

He returns to my side, and I nestle into his arms. He adjusts around me, pulling me close.

"Whoa," he breathes again, a contented tone in his voice.

I don't think I'm going to stop smiling all night.

⌒∾⌒

TIME CREEPS BY, BUT I DON'T WANT TO SLEEP. EXHAUSTION weighs heavy on my body, and my mind is swathed in a downy blanket of bliss, but none of it matters. I don't want to let go of this moment. I'm going to savor it for as long as I can.

My attention slips toward Amar. I don't know if he's asleep. He hasn't moved since we curled up here, his head on my pillows and mine on his chest. His breathing is slow; every time his lungs fill, his skin brushes lightly against my breast.

And like everything else right now, it's wonderful. The simple, soft contact makes me so happy.

I don't even know why.

"Cait?" Amar whispers so softly, I can barely hear him.

I glance up. "Yeah?"

"You're still awake?" He sounds surprised.

My shoulder shrugs.

"You okay?"

I can hear the concern in his voice. I move a bit so I can see him more easily. "Yeah. You?"

He nods, but the question in his eyes doesn't fade.

"It's nothing. Just…" A breath of a chuckle escapes me. "Happy, I guess."

He pauses like he's heard something in my voice. "Okay."

I hesitate too before resting my cheek back against his chest. His hand begins gently stroking my hair.

And I don't know what to say. I *am* happy. Maybe a bit desperately so. I know I should be concerned with all the questions about my mother, about the Touched, about these talents succubi and incubi supposedly have. And I am, somewhere inside. But right now…

Right now I want to lose myself in the feeling that we're normal. Human. That I'm lying in bed with a guy I met in class. That we could go out for a dinner date, or see a movie, or do damn near anything regular people do.

That we could be ordinary.

"What do you want to do after you graduate?" I ask him.

His hand pauses on my hair. "What?"

I shift around on the bed so I can see his face. "After we

graduate," I repeat. "Assuming all of this… I don't know, gets sorted out… What do you want to do?"

He stares at me for a moment like I've taken him aback. And then his lip twitches, his expression pleased and amused at the same time. "Grad school."

"After that."

He hesitates again and then draws a breath like he's prepping himself for my reaction to his answer. "I want to go work in space exploration—or, you know, the research that gets people out there."

My eyebrows climb. I remember he said he was taking quantum physics, back when he saved me from getting caught for nearly killing a guy in the men's room. But I hadn't expected that answer. "Seriously?"

He doesn't respond. I worry I've offended him. "I'm sorry, that came out wrong. I just—"

"It's all right," he says, but his tone is closed off. I can hear it.

"No, it's—" I struggle to explain. "Really, I didn't mean that the way it sounded. I just… I *love* that stuff. Like, Carl Sagan. Arthur C. Clarke. All that. I mean, fantasy was my favorite as a kid. You can't beat Tolkien. And Charles de Lint is amazing. But the idea of space travel—"

I realize I'm babbling, and I cut off. Amar is watching me, though, this funny little smile growing on his lips like he's holding back a laugh. But not at me. Not cruelly, anyway.

"Sorry," I amend, blushing. "I just—"

"Don't apologize. It's great."

The blush grows, and I duck my face away. He catches my chin with his fingertips, pulling my face back toward him gently. "It's great," he insists.

I nod, but I can't help the way my cheeks are still burning. "So how'd you, um… how'd you get into that?"

He hesitates. "My mom."

I freeze, worried that we've stepped onto a landmine of bad memories from his past. He doesn't stop, though.

"When I was little, she gave me a telescope for Christmas. Every night, we'd go up to the roof of our apartment building and try to see the stars past the city lights. But even if we couldn't, she'd still tell me stories about all the worlds that might be out there. Gas giants and diamond planets and places so remote, their sun is just another tiny star. And I…" A faintly embarrassed look flickers over his face. "I fell in love with it. I mean, I knew it was an uphill battle, even then. Black kid, the sciences… Not the, uh, easiest thing." He gives a small scoff like the words are an understatement. "But my mom encouraged me. She believed in me. And now… now I'm here. In college. On my way to grad school. And after that, I want to be a part of finding those places. Maybe even contribute to the research that helps us reach them someday." He falls silent for a moment. "Worlds entirely different than this one."

The implication clicks, and I'm not sure what to say. His words steal my breath and make my heart ache, because I can just picture him. A little boy on a city rooftop, staring at the sky with his mother, dreaming of other worlds.

And I can see the beautiful man who still does, for darker and sadder reasons of his own.

He reaches up, his hand brushing a strand of my hair from my cheek. "Why'd you choose computer science?"

I hesitate. "Computers make sense. People don't."

His smile returns. "I get that."

"I guess I find programming soothing, you know? I

mean, when it's working." I chuckle. He echoes the sound softly. "And creative too. Like… painting with code. Creating something that sort of doesn't exist, but does at the same time. It's like—" I cut off when I realize what I'd been about to say.

"What?" He leans his head to the side, a curious expression on his face while he tries to catch my eye.

"Magic," I finish in a soft voice.

Understanding takes the place of his confusion. He's silent for a moment. "You know the first thing I ever did, back when magic showed up for me?" I start to shake my head, but he doesn't stop. "I broke my little sister's arm."

My eyebrows climb.

"She was barely past being a toddler at the time. We were playing at this park near our apartment building. Just this little scrap of grass and concrete, really, but we had fun. She was chasing me, and I was running—you know, half letting her catch up and then slipping away before she had the chance to reach me. But at some point, I got distracted by these older girls walking past, and she *did* almost grab me. I scrambled to get away, frantic because there was no *way* I was going to let my kid sister actually catch me in front of some pretty girls, right?" His smile lasts only a moment. "But magic came out instead. Rushed from me and shoved her back, making her fall hard. And for a second, I was just frozen. I *felt* it leave me, but I didn't have a clue what had happened, what I'd done. And then she started screaming."

I struggle not to fidget with discomfort. That must have been horrible, for him and her alike. I don't want him to suffer through his bad memories, especially for my sake. But at the same time, he's sharing more with me tonight than he ever has about his past—about *him*, before his biological father came along.

I don't want him to stop even for a moment.

Amar draws a breath. "I... I don't think I'd ever been so scared in my life up till that point, trying to carry her home, worrying every second that cops would show up and think... anything. I had a screaming little girl in my arms, for God's sake. Black kids get shot for *so* much less than that. But I was lucky. I managed to get her home, and my mom and stepdad drove her to the hospital. And my sister kept yelling the whole time that I'd pushed her, that I was horrible and mean and all of that. And I was just dumbstruck. Terrified. I didn't know what to tell them except that it'd been an accident.

"But my stepdad, he took me aside while we were at the hospital. Now, he had no idea what I was—none of them did. But he only had one question for me: had I *meant* to hurt her? I sputtered a defense, how of course I hadn't and all that, and then he stopped me. Asked what was I going to do about it now? And I didn't really have an answer. I told him I'd tell her I was sorry and try to help her get better. Take care of her. Be more careful in the future."

Amar chuckles. "I remember he smiled. Told me that was the crucial part. That what I *did* mattered, but what I did *about* my actions was equally important. People make mistakes, and those have consequences, but if I'd told him the truth and I was willing to do what it took to make things right for her, then that said more about who I was inside than anything else."

He's silent for a moment. "That stayed with me after... after I had to leave. It's not the magic that's evil. Whatever we can do, whatever abilities we might have... it doesn't mean anything about us. It's not who we are. Who we are is what we do with it, and what we do about anything that happens as a result. That's what matters the most."

I nod. I feel like there's something more to the words, though. Like the message isn't *only* about whatever power I might have. Like maybe he's trying to tell me something about himself too.

I just can't quite figure out what it is.

He traces his fingers along my jaw, his eyes tracking the motion. "Can I ask you a question?" he says quietly.

I try not to tense, suddenly wary. "Yeah."

His eyes lift to mine again. "This weekend, would you like to come back to my place?"

I blink, surprised by the shift of topic. "Of course."

He smiles. "I thought we might have dinner—and, you know, whatever else we feel like. Maybe just be ordinary for a while, you know?"

A breath leaves me, bordering on a laugh. "I'd love that."

His smile doesn't fade. "Me too."

I watch him for a moment, grinning, and I don't know what to say. I lay my head back down against his chest.

His hand returns to stroking my hair.

Sleep begins tugging on me. My eyes drift closed. Next weekend… I can't wait. No matter what else is going on, now I have something to look forward to.

It's marvelous.

But I still wonder what he was trying to tell me with his story.

7

AMAR

SHE'S ASLEEP BESIDE HIM, HER HEAD RESTING ON HIS CHEST and her breasts rising and falling with every gentle breath. The night is peaceful, perfect, and fragile like glass. He'd stay in this moment forever if he could.

He wishes it was that simple.

His eyes close. Of all the demons in the world, for her to be Josephine's daughter. It's unthinkable. Horrible.

But he knows what he has to do.

His brow furrows tightly. He's aware that his plan resembles insanity, but he's out of options and has no choice. And he wishes he could explain it to her, but there's too much he doesn't know how to put into words. More than that, though, he knows Cait. She'd never agree, regardless.

She'd insist on coming too.

He looks down at her, lightly running his fingertip across her cheek. Her skin is soft beneath his touch, delicate and beautiful. She stirs against him at the small contact, murmuring contentedly and nestling closer to his side.

Pain moves through him, like an ache burrowing deep into his chest that somehow brings joy too. It's so foreign to him, that feeling. He doesn't want to name it. Doesn't want to admit what it means. And that knowledge doesn't make the pain go away.

Love.

He pulls his hand away with effort. Four little letters. One little word that all of his kind view as a joke, and it's taken him whole. Stolen his heart before he could save himself and claimed him utterly, until he doesn't want an escape.

If he's honest with himself, he never did. Not from her.

Slowly, he lets out a breath. There's a way to keep her out of this. A way to keep her safe. The only one that's left, really. That vampire and troll can't do it. Their plans are madness, and their conspiracy theories of magical Touched are too. But in spite of that, he knows they'll tangle her up in their stories of saving the real Touched and ending the Houses' meat-grinder of human lives. They'll make her believe she can stop a system that's existed for centuries.

They'll get her killed.

But the Houses will do worse. Cait doesn't realize the danger she's in, not really. Alistair, Lucretia, any of the leaders of any House, and all the neutrals out there besides… they'll never let her go. They'll never stop hunting her, not until she's as dead as her mother. He didn't tell Cait the whole story earlier. What Volgert found. What was left of Josephine when her murderers were done with her.

He forces himself to keep breathing. He can't let that happen to Cait. He *won't*.

And he knows what he has to do.
He only hopes she'll understand.

8

The bed doesn't feel right.

My brow furrows against the sensation. I shift around, only to find the other side empty.

I open my eyes, but the rest of the room is empty too. Amar is gone.

Again.

I sigh. Yeah, okay, I admit to myself. I'd hoped he'd be here, since this is my place and Bianca won't find out about us. I'd been sort of looking forward to waking up next to him, seeing as how I've never done that before. Ever. With anyone. Especially him.

I attempt to brush the thought aside. It's fine. Maybe he's just in the living room.

Pushing the blanket away, I sit up only to pause when my eyes catch on a scrap of paper on the nightstand.

Nervousness thrums through me and chokes my throat, owing to the last time I found a note on a tiny piece of paper and all the hell that followed. Eyeing the thing like it might bite, I reach over and pick it up.

Neat handwriting in black ink meets my gaze.

Back soon. Stay safe. -Amar

I bite my lip. I wonder where he's gone.

Setting the note back on my nightstand, I climb out of bed. Yesterday's redecorating has left my room feeling as strange as the rest of the apartment, and I half expect to see entirely new, yet familiar clothes when I open the closet door. Most of my limited wardrobe remains, however. I pull out a shirt and then dig some underwear and a fresh pair of jeans from a drawer. Tossing them all on the bed, I head for the bathroom only to freeze when I see myself in the mirror.

Holy shit, I look like hell.

A grimace twists my face. I pull my attention from my scratched, tousled self. It's nothing a shower won't fix. Well, besides the bruises on my neck and the cuts on my arms, anyhow.

Shivers pebble my skin. I dart into the shower.

Several minutes later finds me dressed, with a scarf added to my outfit to disguise my neck and a long-sleeve shirt covering my arms. Leaving my damp hair down to help conceal my bruises, I brace myself for facing Ruby and walk into the living room.

And then freeze.

Two of the mercenaries are sitting on the couch. The third is in the kitchen. I think he's making coffee.

"Good morning," says one of the pair on the couch. I don't recognize him. Rough-skinned with a long ponytail and a leather vest spiked through with metal studs, he looks like he belongs in a biker bar. Likewise, the auburn-haired woman with him is unfamiliar, as is the dark-haired guy currently sniffing the light roast he found in the kitchen cupboard.

"Hey," I manage, but I can't keep the discomfort from my voice. I haven't actually been alone with them before, I realize. Amar or Brett have always been with me. And yeah, I told Ruby she'd be fine with them here, and I'm sure that's probably right, but—

"What time is your first class?" the guy on the couch asks.

I blink. What?

Oh my God, it's Monday.

My gaze snaps to the clock. Eight forty. My heart slows back toward normal. I'm fine. Class doesn't start till ten.

Are these people going to follow me?

"Um—" I flounder.

"Your friend requested we stay with you." The first guy nods to the man in the kitchen. "He'll watch the other girl."

That answers that question.

"Yeah, all right," I agree for lack of anything else to say. "Uh… my first class is at ten."

He nods. I retreat to my room.

A breath rushes from me after I shut the door. Class. I have to go to class. Listen to a lecture. Take notes.

Pretend I didn't narrowly escape death last night after saving my best friend from the same only a day before.

Easy.

My hand presses to my face like I'm trying to remind myself what's real. Maybe that's why Amar left, though. I never found out his class schedule. It wasn't exactly an important topic in between rescuing Ruby and running for our lives. But that's probably where he is.

God, that man does normal too well.

Struggling to focus, I start away from the door. I don't remember what homework I had. What studying I was supposed to have done. It feels like someone else's life, that world of classes and quizzes and papers from only a few days ago. It's like remembering a foggy dream.

I find my backpack in the corner. My books are inside. A quick check of the calendar on my cell phone reveals I don't have any tests today—a minor miracle, all things considered. Some of my professors are sadists when it comes to Mondays. But regardless, I should be all right.

Except for the werewolves trailing me.

I grimace. It's safer if they do. I get that. It's weird as *hell*, but I get that.

It'll be fine.

I glance around the room, working to make myself believe the words. Amar knows we need the protection. *I* know we need the protection. It's a good thing.

And now I have to pretend like things are normal.

I swallow hard. No problem. Really. No problem at all.

THE WEREWOLVES ARE A PROBLEM.

I hurry across the quad and fight to ignore how people stare at the enormous mercenaries trailing twenty feet behind me. I don't know if anyone has connected me to them; they've stayed several yards back the whole day. But they aren't exactly hiding either.

And with their black leather clothes, predatory body language, and builds like a pair of fricking *Vikings*, they're damn near impossible to miss.

I grimace when I reach my car. Visibility is the point, I realize that. Even if the humans don't understand what these people are doing here, any demons will get the message. But it's still been nerve-wracking, like a constant reminder that my life might be in danger. That no matter how it looks on the outside, things are most decidedly *not* normal. I figured getting back to school and pretending everything was fine would be hard, but the mercenaries have made it so much worse.

They followed me to class. They sat in the backs of lecture halls, their weirdly intent gazes practically daring anyone to talk to me. They trailed me to discussion sections, thankfully staying outside the classrooms but lingering in places where they could see me through the windows or open doors the whole time. I managed to keep them from accompanying me to the restroom, but that was about my only victory for the day.

God, I wish I knew where to find Amar.

I let out a breath in frustration. At the sound, the werewolves stop on their way to their motorcycles and turn immediately, looking to me in unison in that creepy manner they have. I work to hide my reaction.

I'm not fast enough.

They come toward me. I tense, but there isn't anywhere to go.

"Everything all right?" the guy with the ponytail asks, his voice low. He and his companion tower above me, for all that they're no taller than Amar. But Amar never made me nervous like this. I suddenly feel like a little kid trapped between a couple of very large adults.

Adults with weird amber eyes that remind me of a wild animal's gaze, even if I can't put my finger on why.

"Yeah." I nod quickly. "Totally."

He pauses. I can tell he doesn't believe me.

"Listen," I try. "You guys could probably—"

"Four demons passed by your twelve o'clock class," he interrupts me smoothly. "Two more attempted to slip in the back of the restaurant where you had lunch. Three have been spotted near your friend. It is better that the lackeys of the Houses see us. It makes them question how many of us they *haven't* seen."

My mouth moves. Words don't come out.

"You are not the one paying us, miss," he reminds me. "We have to do our job."

Air escapes me. I'm not sure what to say.

They head for their bikes.

"Could you just—" I start.

The guy looks at me.

I try to find a way to explain. "Listen, I don't even know your names, okay? You're ghosting along behind me, and I—"

He glances at his companion. They walk back toward me.

"My name is Ulric." He tilts his head toward his companion. "This is Sorcha."

The cinnamon-haired woman nods in greeting. She's easily the same height as Ulric, and she looks muscular enough that I wouldn't know which of them to put money on in a fight.

I echo the motion nervously. "I'm Cait. Were you at the…" I hesitate, my eyes darting around to check if anyone's close enough to overhear. "You know, that thing the other night?"

"Yes."

I fight the urge to swallow anxiously. I'd seen them, then. Blood on their fur. On their teeth. They'd been terrifying.

They'd made it possible to save Ruby.

"Thank you for helping us," I say, my words rushed.

"It's what we were paid to do."

I don't know how to respond. There's nothing in his words. We might as well be discussing the delivery of a pizza.

"You should get back to your apartment," Sorcha tells me. Her voice is gentler than I would have imagined, coming from someone who looks like she could snap me in half. "It's safer there."

I nod and reach for the door handle. They start toward their bikes again.

Another thought hits me.

"I'm sorry," I say.

They glance back.

"About the others. Your..." I flounder. They're mercenaries. Brett made it clear they don't give a crap about anybody, and Ulric's words sort of just proved that.

I still feel like I should say something.

"Your friends or..." I shrug awkwardly. "Whoever they were. The ones who didn't make it. I'm sorry."

For the longest moment, they don't move, and then Ulric's brow twitches down slightly, like he's surprised by what I said. He nods once before heading for his bike.

Sorcha watches me a heartbeat more. I can't tell what I'm seeing in her eyes.

"My brothers," she says quietly.

Words fail me all over again.

She returns to her motorcycle. I stare after her, feeling a bit like I've been punched in the gut. Her brothers? Oh my God...

I manage to climb into the car. It takes me a moment to collect myself enough to remember how to drive.

The apartment is silent when I arrive, and Ruby's bedroom door is open, making it obvious she's not home.

"Your roommate is studying at the library," Ulric supplies.

I freeze, suddenly wondering if telepathy is part of their abilities.

"The night watch will be here in a couple hours," Sorcha adds. "Do you have anywhere you need to be this evening? Any plans they should be aware of?"

I shake my head. "N-no. I don't think so."

She nods. Ulric moves to the window and tugs back the curtains, scanning the street outside, while Sorcha walks around the apartment, her amber gaze sweeping the walls and ceiling like she's checking something.

I glance between them. Okay, then.

I escape into my room and dump my backpack on the floor while the door shuts behind me. For a moment, I just stand there.

Now what?

A breath leaves me. I can't call Amar. I want to, but in the hubbub of staying alive this weekend, I'd never asked for his number. Or Bianca's. Or anyone's.

I kick myself internally. Of all the things to slip my mind…

But I could call Temptation. That information should be easy enough to find online. And Brett should have Amar's number, assuming he's around at this hour.

I dig my cell phone out. My internet browser is painfully slow, but it turns up the number for the night-club eventually.

I raise the phone to my ear. Several rings pass, and I'm about to hang up when finally the ringing cuts off.

"Temptation."

"Uh, hi. Is this Brett?"

"Who is this?"

"Cait. You remember? From yesterday? I, uh—"

"Yeah, I remember you. What's up?"

I exhale, struggling to regroup. "I wondered if I could get Amar's number from you."

"He didn't give you his number?"

"No, I didn't get a chance to ask him for—"

I hear a noise in the background on the other end of the line. "Yeah, hey, I'll sign for those in a second." Brett's voice is muffled like he put a hand to the phone. "Listen," he continues to me. "I've got to go. Just ask him whenever he gets back from class or whatever."

"Well, but—"

The line clicks.

For a moment, I don't move. Seriously?

I lower the cell. Dammit, *now* what?

Grimacing, I set my phone on the desk. Now nothing. Ruby's at the library. I hate that I'm almost relieved by that. And Amar…

Amar is fine. Brett's right. I'll get his number when he comes back. I'm just keyed up from the weekend. Being paranoid. His absence doesn't mean anything is wrong.

I haul my backpack over to my bed and start to take out my books. I hope he meant it when he said he'd be back soon.

9

AMAR

HOURS HAVE PASSED SINCE HE CALLED IN THE FAVORS HE needed to find her current location. It may be approaching a full day. Time is impossible to tell in the windowless cavern of the antechamber, where the cold air is motionless and chilled by the black marble until it feels like a tomb. But for two chairs of dark wood against one wall, and a door of equally dark wood on the opposite, the room is featureless. He has stood inside it since he arrived, waiting.

It's a message. He realizes that. He wouldn't have expected anything else.

A click sounds in the silence. He glances at the door, watching while it swings open. Two men step through, both dressed in suits. In silence, they take up positions on either side of the entryway. He strides between them from the room. The men follow.

His footsteps echo in the stillness while he walks down the long corridor. At least there are windows here, a small way to determine how long he's waited. Past the tall, arched casements, he can see the night sky and the silver-touched fields and forests that surround the manor. The road away from this place is a pale ribbon in the moonlight; no cars are on it.

Expressionless, he returns his attention to the corridor. Nighttime, then, but with dawn approaching in not too much longer by the look of it. After so many years of living as an incubus, he has a near-instinctive sense of time at night, though it helps to see the sky. It's been at least sixteen hours since the end of the long drive that brought him to this place.

He wonders if Cait has started to question where he's gone.

The thought is dismissed swiftly. He can't think about that right now.

A door at the end of the corridor opens, revealing a slender maid with dark hair, snow-pale skin, and red eyes. She bows her head quickly, stepping aside. He walks into the room, a brief flick of his gaze taking in the crimson curtains, the dark furniture. An ornate chandelier hangs from the ceiling, complete with burning candles coated in drips of pale wax. Thick tapestries drape the corners of the room—obscuring bodyguards, he's sure. Overall, the effect is classic. One could almost say stereotypical. Volgert has always tended more toward the gothic—unlike the Al Capone-era style of Linden or the near-obsession with modernity found in some of the other Houses—but even by that standard, the atmosphere is practically medieval.

And it's a ruse. An illusion designed to make other demons underestimate her, to make them dismiss her as an old romantic clinging to bygone days, and forget that her holdings exceed those of a Wall Street titan while her influence extends across whole continents and oceans. He knows she enjoys using the trick, perhaps more than any other in her arsenal.

Lucretia turns from the small table in the center of the room, her brow rising in feigned astonishment as if he's arrived unexpectedly. A black dress covers her, from the tight collar reaching up to her pale jawline down to the flowing skirt obscuring her ankles. Her dark, glossy hair is swept up and fastened by jewel-studded clasps that glint in the candlelight. A rich red ruby hangs from a burnished chain at her throat. Her equally red lips curl into a pleased smile at the sight of him, revealing white teeth without a hint of fangs. She appears to be in her mid-thirties. Perhaps forty at the outside.

But he knows she's far older.

"Well, now," she says. "This is a pleasant surprise. How long has it been, Amar? Five years? Six?"

He's silent. She's aware of the math as much as he is.

Lucretia's smile broadens. "And to what do I owe the pleasure of this visit?"

"I think you know."

Her expression turns disingenuous. "I do?"

He resumes his silence. So that was how it was going to be. He'd mostly expected it. Games were how Lucretia kept the centuries from becoming dull.

True to form, she gives him a humored look. "Oh, Amar. All this time, and still, you haven't developed even the *slightest* sense of humor. You could have at least tried to pick *that* up from your father, you know. No matter what you think of him, surely not all of his traits were bad ones?"

She chuckles when he doesn't reply. Turning, she

regards the small, round table at the center of the room again. Atop the red tablecloth, a tall vase holds a bouquet of dark roses. With slender fingers, she selects one and draws it out.

"So what *is* this reason of which I'm supposedly already aware?" She studies the flower contemplatively.

"Cait."

Her brow rises. "Who?"

He doesn't respond. She smiles.

"Is this the young lady with whom you showed up at the set the other night?"

"The one your people have been harassing for days, yes."

She scoffs lightly. "My people have been harassing *Linden*. I'll admit to that. And we have a very specific reason for doing so." Her smile returns. "But how has this become *your* problem?"

He considers his answer, aware that the question is loaded.

In so many ways.

"Linden is irrelevant," he replies. "Whatever issue you have with them is as well. But Cait isn't involved with Linden. She wants nothing to do with them."

Lucretia looks surprised. "Oh, really? How intelligent of her."

"Cait's a neutral. She's not interested in being a part of the Houses, nor in aiding one of them against any others. Because of that, I'm asking you to leave her alone."

"And if I don't?"

His heart does not begin to pound harder. His breathing remains steady. The slightest change would be a clear sign of stress, and she'd pick up on every one.

But he's good at this.

"Then you would be putting our agreement at risk."

Her brow rises, and a tapestry stirs in the corner. He doesn't look away from her, but the motion confirms his suspicion.

They're not alone.

"If you cannot leave a neutral out of this who is determined to stay out, then how am I to trust that our agreement will stand?" he continues calmly.

"You and I have a very *special* arrangement, Amar," she points out, "owing to the deep affection I had for your father, and to the fact that neither you nor I are particularly suicidal. It has nothing to do with this girl or anyone else in the demonic world."

She turns and paces away, twirling the rose between her fingertips, and he can read the action. Despite her words, she's putting distance between them, daring him to try anything.

And leaving space for her people to shoot him, in case he does.

"I miss your father," Lucretia muses. "So strong. So sensual. So *unusual*—like you." She glances over her shoulder to him. "Does she know about you, this girl you seem to have—what? Taken under your wing? Have you told her the truth of what you are?"

He doesn't respond.

"I'll take that as a no, then. And why is that, Amar? Someone for whom you're suddenly so willing to jeopardize our agreement... Surely, you trust her?" Lucretia's smile deepens. It reminds him of a cobra. "My own sweet Josephine, returned to me in the form of her daughter."

He watches her, evaluating. It hadn't really been a question, whether or not Lucretia knew about Cait's mother. The only question had been whether she'd choose to be the one to bring it up first.

And to what end.

Lucretia returns her attention to the rose. "I cannot begin to describe what I felt when my people reported the arrival of the two of you at the set the other night. Your presence alone would have been worthy of comment, but her?" She shakes her head as if in awe. "Incredible."

"And you knew nothing of her before then."

She gives him a look like, if she were human, she'd sigh. "Sadly, no. The agents I have harassing Linden were not familiar with her mother, and regardless, they did not report Cait's appearance. They said only that Alistair had acquired another Legacy who hadn't shown up till recently. An anomaly, if you will. If it weren't that she appears so similar to Josephine she could have stepped from a *photograph* of her mother, I doubt we'd know who she was even now."

"Then call your people off now," he replies, the words measured.

"Is that really the best approach, Amar? Cait isn't like you. She doesn't have your gifts. And you can't be around all the time."

His eyes narrow.

"That wasn't a threat," she assures him patiently. "Merely a statement of fact. Even if you *do* try to protect her, even if she *is* uninterested in joining Linden as you say, she will still need friends in this world."

"She doesn't require that friend to be you."

Lucretia laughs. "She hasn't even *met* me. How can you be so sure we wouldn't get along?"

Her humor deepens into pity at his silence. "Oh Amar, you know it doesn't need to be this way. You, out on your own, with nothing but some fragile alliance with that Chastain family between you and utter isolation. And they don't even know what you are, do they? Not really. No, it's only you out there. My dear boy with the power so terrible, he hides it even from himself for fear of what he knows he could do."

She crosses back toward him. "I told you all those years ago: I have no opposition to you having the life you want. A college degree. An ordinary job. A *mostly* ordinary life. All those things could still be yours, but you could have protection and safety too. You and this girl both." She reaches up, touching his cheek in a maternal gesture. "Would that be so terrible?"

He turns his face slightly. She lets her hand fall away.

"No, my dear. I'm sorry, but I cannot in good conscience leave Cait out there too, not with circumstances as they are. My people are harrying Linden for a very good reason—one that threatens Cait equally as much as me." Her brow rises, her expression projecting curiosity. "Or did Alistair not say anything about that when he brought you in to speak with him the other day?"

His gaze meets hers. "Was it me or him you had under surveillance?"

She appears amused. "I have to pick just one?"

He doesn't answer.

Lucretia's smile remains. "Him. Mostly. Though it was alarming to hear you'd been brought in so easily."

"They found me at school."

"Ah." She nods. "Messy. Of course." She paces away and lays the dark rose on the red tablecloth. "Alistair Linden has become rather more of a threat as of late, and now he has something I want. Something that means my people, your ostensible 'friends,' and even Cait are in danger." She pauses, glancing back at him. "And something she can assist me in finding."

He doesn't react despite how the words confirm what he'd been concerned is true.

Lucretia already has plans for Cait.

"There are Touched," she continues, "who aren't like the others. Special and *rare* beyond belief, rather like yourself—though sadly none have displayed *your* specific abilities. But with magical talents like incubi and succubi."

Her eyes narrow when he remains silent. "You knew about this, didn't you?" She laughs. "Oh, Amar, I've missed you. How much have you heard?"

"Only that."

Her brow shrugs. "Well, this *particular* Touched is also something of an anomaly, like you and Cait. They have a power unlike any that has been found in the demonic world in… well, centuries, in this case."

"What kind of power?"

"Psychic."

He allows his skepticism to show.

"It seems impossible, I realize. Thankfully, the ability seems limited and sporadic—otherwise, I have no doubt we would all already be dead. But it is true. Now, I have tried persuasion. I have tried force. But Alistair refuses to give the Touched up, and all the pressure my people brought to bear in the few short weeks since he discovered this person has been unsuccessful in changing his mind. However, my agents have uncovered information leading me to believe he may be hiding this individual among the regular Touched, and this is where Cait comes in. My agents would secure her access to Linden's stock—in total safety, of course. She would identify the one he is hiding, and my people would take care of the rest. The threat ends."

"Cait is not your pawn."

"*Ally*," she corrects as if wounded. "Please, Amar. I wouldn't do such a thing to her."

He regards the vampire for a long moment. "No. Cait stays out of this, Lucretia. I stay out of it. Your people leave her and all her friends and family alone, and you find this Touched another way."

His gaze slides to the tapestries, where he knows bodyguards are hiding, and he's aware of the message he's making clear in the motion. Without another word, he turns and heads for the door.

"I could force the issue."

He looks back. Lucretia's smile is gone. Something else remains, tense and mostly hidden. On anyone else, he'd swear it was fear.

"You are a special case," she says. "And we both know how precarious this deal of ours could be."

She walks toward him. "If this Touched of Alistair's has a vision of Cait, how long do you think she'll survive? How tolerant of her *neutrality* do you think he will be? A single look at her, and Alistair must have known whose daughter she is. The only reason he has not simply *forced* her into his House at gunpoint *must* be because he suspects she's a Trojan horse of my own making. But what happens if his little psychic sees otherwise?" Lucretia makes a disgusted sound. "And what about the Chastain family?" Her gaze scrapes over him. "What about *you*? One shot, darling. Alistair and the rest who are aware of what you are, they know they'll only get one, and if they miss, they're done. But what could they do if that psychic happens to predict *precisely* where and when that shot needs to be taken?"

He doesn't answer, and after a moment, she straightens like she's collecting herself. "I'll deal about Cait on one condition. You."

"No."

Something ugly twists through Lucretia's expression. "Then you will watch me *break* that child. You will watch me shred her world and slaughter every single person who means a *damn* to her. And if you try to stop me, if you *kill* me, I will still have as many people sent after you as it takes to get that one shot in."

A quiver runs through her like she's fighting to get herself back under control, but slowly, calm reasserts itself over her face. She leans closer, and when she speaks, her voice is low, as if she's trying to keep anyone from hearing. "You and I both know you don't want me as an enemy, Amar. And I don't want you as one either. Find this Touched. Remove them from Alistair's hands one way or another, but help me keep that fool from destroying our world. And then—" She seems to struggle with the words. "And then we will discuss Cait's situation."

He studies her, unmoving. She's desperate, he realizes. The leader of one of the most powerful Houses in the demonic world, and she's absolutely desperate.

And he doesn't imagine for a moment that she won't do everything she's threatened for Cait and more.

He fights back a grimace. This is suicide. Or damn near as close to it as he's ever wanted to come. Every instinct for survival he has is screaming for him to walk away.

And by the time he returned to the apartment, Cait would have been taken and Ruby would be dead. Every security measure he put in place wouldn't be a match for an all-out assault ordered by the leader of a House.

The plan to come here had been desperate too.

"Your people don't touch her," he says, his voice equally soft. "They back off, and they keep any other House from coming near Cait, her friends, or her family at the same time."

She nods once. "Agreed."

He hesitates for a heartbeat, weighing whether to trust the fast reply and whether it wouldn't be better to have a backup plan in place.

Just in case.

"And when the situation with this Touched is over," he continues. "I leave. Our deal resumes—and it covers Cait too."

She's silent. Her jaw works around like she's trying to decide how to respond.

"Cait doesn't want this, Lucretia. She doesn't want her powers or anything to do with this world." He pauses. "She's not Josephine. She never will be."

Her mouth tightens. "Very well."

"Thank you."

Lucretia glances up at him, and after a moment, a hint of her smile returns. "We really would make a good team, you know," she murmurs.

He meets her eyes flatly.

Her smile broadens. "Ah well." She walks back to the table and takes up the rose again. "My people will escort you to a room where you may stay. I'll have someone bring you up some nourishment as well. You'll leave with my agents for the nearest Linden storage of Touched this evening after sunset."

He heads for the door.

"It's a pleasure to have you back again, Amar."

He glances over his shoulder.

"Even if only for now," she amends.

Without a word, he leaves the room, hoping he's not making a mistake.

Desperately.

10

Sunlight creeps across my walls, and I blink when I realize I've been staring at shadow lines cast by my window blinds. I don't know how long they've been there or when they went from darkness to a shape on my wall, but I grimace, rolling away from the sight.

So much for getting to sleep before dawn.

I scrub a hand over my face. It's ridiculous. *I'm* ridiculous. But a whole night of that knowledge hasn't made sleep arrive any quicker. Or at all.

In frustration, I shove my blankets aside. It's not just that Amar hasn't returned or that I can't stop worrying something happened to him and I'd never know. After all, it's not like Bianca would tell me.

Hell, the girl probably wouldn't think to tell *anyone*.

My stomach roils. It's not only that, though. Ruby didn't come home till after midnight, and like a coward, I couldn't even make myself go out to see her. I know she's got to be going through hell right now. I know this isn't just about me and that, even if it's hard, I need to be there for her. But I didn't want to deal with that look on her face again. The one that says I might be a monster.

The one that makes me worry she might be right.

I climb to my feet and stalk toward the closet, resolutely trying to ignore the way my legs shake. It's back, the craving. The hunger. Back like floodwaters lapping at the edge of my mind, inching closer until they can swallow me whole. And I don't know what to do about it. Or rather, I know *exactly* what I need to do about it.

But I don't want to.

I take a shirt from a hanger and keep my breathing steady while I put it on. I'll be fine, though. Amar will be too.

Wherever the hell he is.

I scowl. Amar isn't my boyfriend—and even if he was, it'd be the acme of stupidity to need to know where he was at every hour of the damn day. I'm not like that.

And he is *fine*. Safe. He can take care of himself.

I hope.

Resolutely, I draw another breath. Ridiculous. Totally ridiculous.

I'd feel a lot better if I stopped by his place, though. Made sure and all that.

I pause, my eyes darting to the clock. That could work, actually. I still have a few hours until class. And I remember his address from when we left his apartment the other day.

It'll be easy.

I head for the living room before I can start talking myself out of the idea.

The lights aren't on and the blinds are closed, casting the living room in a dim twilight. But the werewolves are still here. They glance over when I open the door, and their eyes glint brightly in the shadows.

I freeze.

The weird reflectivity in their eyes vanishes, leaving three ordinary-looking Vikings sitting on the couch and armchair in my living room.

"Hello," the nearest one comments.

They look away before I can respond, their gazes fastening on the door like they heard something, and one of them rises from his seat. He crosses the room and pulls the door open.

Sorcha, Ulric, and the other guy from yesterday are standing there. Without a word, they step past the man by the door, though Ulric gives him a brief nod of acknowledgment.

The other two on the couch stand up. "See you this evening," one says to me.

They file from the apartment.

"Early morning today?" Ulric asks me. He sounds like he's making a note of my schedule for future reference.

My mouth moves. "Um, no. I mean, yeah, but not for class. I—" An awkward feeling hits me. "I was going to stop by Amar's apartment first."

Nothing changes in his expression. "Leaving now?"

"Yeah."

Sorcha turns and walks back into the hall while Ulric steps aside, clearing a path for me to follow her. "He'll watch your friend, same as yesterday."

Ulric nods to the man with them.

I hesitate. "Okay." I slip past Ulric and the other guy into the hallway. Sorcha is already by the stairs. I wonder what the neighbors will think if they see me with these massive bodyguards for the second day in a row.

The mercenaries trail me all the way to Amar's building, parking only one spot behind me when I find a place on the street. I bite my lip while I get out of the car. They'll want to come with me upstairs. They'll probably insist on it.

For that matter, I doubt I stand a chance of convincing them to do otherwise.

With the two of them flanking me like a bizarre entourage, I wait by the locked entrance for someone to leave the building and then slip in before the glass door can close. The lobby is empty, thankfully, and the elevator is as well. In silence, I stand in the small confines, watching the numbers creep upward, with the two werewolves on either side of me. I know I'm probably safe with them. Safer than I would be *without* them, anyway. But it's still a struggle to keep that image from my mind, the one from the set when they were in their other form, and all the damage they did that night.

The elevator dings. I stride out quickly when the door pulls back.

Amar's floor appears empty. Thick carpet muffles the sound of my footsteps and obliterates Sorcha's and Ulric's passage completely. It amazes me how silent the two of them are. The bright lights around us eliminate any chance at shadows. Along the cream-colored walls, dark wooden doors stand at long distances from one another; indications, I suppose, of the size of the apartments they hide.

I round the corner and continue down the hall. Amar's apartment is near the corner of the building. I'm pretty sure I remember the number.

My footsteps slow when I near his door, and nervously, I cast a brief look at Sorcha and Ulric.

Without a word, Sorcha slips past me and Amar's door

alike and takes up a position closer to the fire exit at the end of the hall. Ulric hangs back, keeping watch on the other stretch of the corridor.

I swallow hard. Okay, here goes nothing. Taking a deep breath, I lift my hand to knock.

What if he's with someone in there?

I freeze at the sudden thought. What if that's why he left the other night? Because he needed to feed off somebody after everything we'd been through.

Air escapes me. That's okay. That's not so horrible. I mean, it makes my stomach try to twist through itself in complete violation of the laws of physics, but it's better than any other alternative—like him being hurt or dead. Maybe he's simply been distracted, making up for the energy we can't give each other.

My hand lowers. It's hard to breathe. The hall feels too cramped, and I know I must look like an idiot to Ulric and Sorcha, but now I'm worried Amar will open the door. Find me out here, with him standing in the doorway with a sheet around his waist or those drawstring pants he wore the other day. And it's fine. I mean, it's really fine. We can't get the energy we need from each other, so of course he'll need to sleep with other people. I know that. I will soon too, for pity's sake. And that… that's fine.

I'm frozen like a deer in headlights, and I don't know what to do.

"Cait."

I jump a mile. My gaze snaps over to find Ulric striding toward me, a murderous expression on his face. "We need to go," he orders. "Now."

I look between him and Sorcha, who's motioning urgently for me to head for the emergency exit. Confused, I start toward her, anxiety beginning to gallop through me.

I haven't heard anything. Seen anything. The hallway seems exactly—

"Hey, don't go rushing off on my account."

My heart leaps into my throat, but Ulric moves fast, putting himself between me and the origin of the voice before I can even turn. A wave of hostility comes off the werewolf like a wall. I retreat in spite of myself.

I catch sight of the person beyond him. Ram stands at the corner of the hallway, regarding us with an amused expression.

"So that's all you've got, eh? Two mercenary pups. And here, of all places." He shakes his head. "You really don't know what you're up against, do you?"

Ulric gestures sharply for me to go toward Sorcha, not taking his eyes from Ram.

"Oh, come on," Ram chides.

The emergency exit door opens. A guy built like a six-foot-tall brick steps through. He's big like Ram, like a boulder, with dark skin and shoulders that barely fit through the doorframe. I think he might be another troll.

Sorcha stops at the sight of him. A growl leaves her, low and chilling. The hairs on my arms stand on end. There's nothing human in that sound.

"How many times do I have to tell you I don't want any trouble?" Ram sighs.

I look between them, not sure what to do. But we're trapped. I haven't got a clue what trolls can do, but it's not hard to guess that it can't be good. Otherwise, I don't doubt that Sorcha or Ulric would've already gotten me out of here.

So fighting's out, and that leaves talking—something at which I'm not that great. But it's all we've got.

"Try a few more," I retort, mustering up as much bravado as I can.

"We're looking out for you, Cait."

"Funny way of showing it." I glance at the other guy. "Back off. I don't intend to have any conversations here. You want to talk, we do it someplace else."

Ram chuckles. "Okay, sure. We could talk. Not really why we're here, though."

I tense.

"Amar isn't home, is he?"

Wary alarm prickles in my veins.

"He's gone back to Volgert," Ram elaborates. "Went back to Lucretia the minute he left your apartment the other night, and he's been at her place ever since."

"You're lying."

"Our people kept an eye on him. Spies reported his arrival minutes after he got there." Ram shakes his head. "I tried to tell you: be careful who you trust."

My heart is thudding so hard I'm sure the wolves can hear it. "Get out of our way."

Ram glances instead to Ulric and Sorcha. "So *he* paid these two to guard you? You sure they aren't just keeping an eye on you for Volgert?"

A growl leaves Ulric this time. "Watch yourself, troll."

Ram grins briefly, his metal teeth flashing in the light. "I'm here to help you, Cait. Help you join up with the *real* neutrals and maybe do some good in this world. Amar lied. He's carrying on like he actually managed to leave the Houses behind, but it's bullshit. Someone like him, someone with *his* history?" He shakes his head. "Wouldn't happen. I mean, do you even know who he *is*?"

I can't help it. I recoil like I'm trying to put distance between myself and the words.

"Yeah. Didn't think so. Amar's a monster every bit as bad as his father. Everyone knows that. And the rumors of what he can do, what they *both* could do..." Ram chuckles. The sound sends shivers swarming over my skin. "Story is, Amar even took the guy out. Did he tell you that? He was all set to follow in his father's footsteps, trained up like a right old apprentice to the mantle. Then suddenly, his daddy's dead, and Amar simply strolls out of the sadistic bastard's sworn House. Says he's neutral, and Lucretia Volgert doesn't make a peep. Neither do any of the other Houses. Hell, Lucretia even forbade any of her people from *asking* him about it."

"He made a deal with her," I say, but my voice isn't as firm as before. "Promised to stay out of anything to do with the Houses."

"Oh yeah, like *that'd* ever work. And look what a great job he's done at it too. Talking with Alistair. Walking into a set the other night. Getting involved with you. And now he's gone back to meet the matriarch of Volgert. Some deal."

I'm silent.

"He's not in this to help you, Cait. Amar and Lucretia have an arrangement, sure, but it's not for him to be neutral. Not by far."

I shake my head. I know he's got to be wrong. Got to be lying.

His face isn't saying that, though.

"Our people can protect you," Ram insists. "Not like the Houses. Not with lifetime agreements trapping you. We can help because it's the right thing to do and because you can save lives. That's all we're interested in." He pauses. "You tell me if you think I'm lying."

I shudder harder at the repetition of my own thoughts.

At how I can't quite convince myself he's not telling the truth.

There has to be more to it, though. There just *has* to be.

I move toward Amar's door, never taking my eyes from him. Ulric comes too, keeping himself between me and Ram. I raise my fist and knock on Amar's door.

Ram sighs.

But nothing else happens.

I knock again.

"He's gone to—"

I make a hard noise. Ram cuts off.

Seconds creep past. No one answers the door.

I shiver. Amar has to have a good reason for this. For everything.

No matter what Ram says.

"Let's go," I tell Ulric, my voice tight.

He nods. I march toward Sorcha, doing everything I can to appear threatening to the enormous troll blocking our way to the stairs.

The guy smirks and then looks beyond us to Ram.

"Come on, Cait," Ram chides. "Let us help you. You're not going to be able to stay out of this forever—especially with Amar setting you up for Volgert."

I reach the other troll. "Move."

The man makes a small grunt of amusement.

Tingles run through me, and purple mist rises from my fists to tangle like smoke around my arms. I fight not to let on that it scares me, that I don't have the first *clue* what I'm doing, or that the magic could die at any moment based on how little of it I probably have in me right now. I stare into his eyes instead. "Now."

"Tank," Ram calls.

The guy looks at him again and then steps aside.

I stride past him and down the steps, struggling the whole while to make the magic on my hands disappear without blowing something up unintentionally. Sorcha and Ulric follow me. The door swings shut behind them, and the mist fades.

My strength goes with it.

With a gasp, I collapse against the banister, my legs suddenly unable to hold me. The stairwell swirls like it's caught in a blender, and it's all I can do to hang onto the railing until the world slows back toward normal.

"Are you all right?"

I blink to find Sorcha crouched on the steps in front of me, her hand hovering near my shoulder like she wants to steady me but is afraid to touch me at the same time. Alarm shows in her amber eyes.

Swallowing hard, I nod.

"What—" Sorcha starts.

"When's the last time you fed?" Ulric asks.

I falter, unsure what to say. That sort of doesn't feel like his business.

But then, I did just collapse in front of him.

"Don't know," I manage. "Few days ago, I think. A little bit."

He lets out a breath. I see Sorcha glance at him from the corner of my eye.

"Can you walk?" Ulric asks.

I nod and hope I'm telling the truth. My legs feel like they're made of water. My whole body feels like it's going to rattle apart. Drawing a deep breath, I hoist myself up by the railing.

My muscles quiver, but they hold. I start down the steps, bracing myself on the banister.

"Take the door to the next level," Ulric instructs.

Sorcha nods. She hurries down the steps two at a time, and then tugs open the fire door when she reaches it.

I trail them down a hallway that's nearly identical to the one we just left. Sorcha strides ahead and summons the elevator.

They don't say a word while we ride to the first floor with me clinging to the railing to keep myself steady. When we arrive, I hurry out the door as fast as my legs will carry me, avoiding the odd looks we receive from the few people lingering in the lobby. I just want to get to my car because I can guess the question that is coming, and I don't want to deal with it. I'll figure this out, and without two werewolves basically chaperoning the whole damn thing.

Ulric stops when we reach the street. "For your safety, your classes should wait till you have fed at a protected location. Where may we take you to—"

My phone buzzes, making me jump. I scramble to dig it from my pocket. I don't want to answer what I know Ulric's about to ask me.

I glance at the number briefly, and surprise flares through me when I recognize it. Quickly, I answer the call. "Hello?"

"Hey, Cait? It's Brett. You home?"

Tension creeps through me. "Uh, no... Why?"

"All right, look, Amar just called."

"What? Is he okay?"

"Huh?" Brett sounds thrown by the concern in my voice. "Yeah, he's fine. But he said there's some shit going on right now that's, um... he'd like it if you and that girl from the other night could come stay at my place for a while. Over at Temptation."

I blink, confused. "What's going on?"

"It's Houses shit."

I'm not certain how to respond. "But what—"

"Just find your friend and head over soon as you can. He thinks it'd be safer if you were here."

"Okay, but—"

Ulric takes the phone from me. "We'll be there within the hour." He hangs up.

I gape at him. "*Excuse* me. Just what the hell—"

"We were hired to keep you safe," he points out levelly. "This is how." He glances around the street. "And the club will have food for you."

I swallow hard. Food. Awesome. *Not* the way I would have described it.

Ulric hands the phone back to me and then strides toward my car. Sorcha nods for me to follow him.

I'm not sure what to do. Arguing won't go well. It won't go anywhere at all.

And if Amar *did* call… if he really *does* want me to stay at Temptation instead of my apartment, despite all the security he's already got in place…

I don't care what Ram said. Amar is trustworthy. So there has to be a good reason. A *damn* good one, actually.

This is Amar we're talking about.

I head for the car.

11

I come to a stop in front of my apartment and feel like I'm seeing some flashback to yesterday.

Mostly because there's a moving van in the driveway again.

The movers give the mercenaries beside me odd looks when we walk past. I continue upstairs, only to find the front door to my apartment open. Men with safety braces strapped around their backs and chests are hefting boxes out the door.

"Hey!" I hurry toward them. "What are you—"

"No, not that stuff."

I cut off at the sound of Ruby's voice. The movers shift aside to give me room when I push past them on my way down the hall. Sorcha and Ulric follow me, watching everyone like they're weighing whether or not to attack.

Ruby is standing by her bedroom. She doesn't look over when I come to the front door. A pair of smaller plastic bins sit beside her, and she nods when a mover bends to lift them both. "Yeah," she continues. "That should be all of it."

I step aside numbly while the man carries the boxes toward the hall.

"Ruby?" I try.

She retreats into her bedroom without a word.

A rough breath leaves me. I don't... she can't...

What the *hell*?

Incredulous, I stride over to the door. She's standing in the middle of the empty room. The string of snapshots is missing from her wall, and the hangers in her closet are empty. A suitcase rests on the floor, clothes already folded inside.

"What is this?" I demand.

She's silent.

"Ruby, what the hell is—"

"I can't do this, Cait. I-I can't stay here. Can't..."

She looks back at me, and I can see her shaking. Her voice seems barely this side of controlled. Dark circles are painted beneath her eyes like bruises.

I suddenly wonder how long it's been since she slept.

Flabbergasted, I start toward her. "Ruby—"

She flinches, and her hand flies up, motioning me to stop. "Don't."

I freeze. The fear that flashed across her face feels like a dagger in my chest.

She draws a ragged breath. "I'm leaving."

"What?"

"I-I've withdrawn from classes. Told the college I had a family emergency. But I've got to go."

"But—" I glance at the living room. The movers are mostly gone. Ulric and Sorcha are standing with the other werewolf by the door. From the sound of it, Ulric is chewing him out for not calling to warn them about this. "But what about what Amar said? The side effects? The people who'll—"

She shakes her head, cutting me off. "I don't care. I'm going home to Mom's place in Arizona."

A breath escapes me. "But—"

"I'm leaving, Cait!"

I blink at the shout.

She turns away. With unsteady hands, she zips up her suitcase.

My mouth moves, searching for words, and my voice is small when I find them. "When are you coming back?"

She doesn't respond.

A knock comes on the door. "Hello?"

"In here, Oliver," Ruby calls, not looking away from her bag.

I turn, speechless, as her brother appears at the door. Oliver is nineteen and a freshman in college, but he still hasn't outgrown the gawky little-kid look—though the mop of unruly dark hair falling into his eyes doesn't really help.

But he's supposed to be at school in Arizona. He goes to college in the same town where their mom lives. And if he's here…

My God, when did Ruby call her family? When did she start planning this?

"Uh—" Oliver gives Ulric and the others a wary look and then continues past them. "Hey, Cait." He flashes me a brief smile, but his attention immediately returns to his sister. I can't imagine what she told her family—I doubt it was the truth—but it's easy to see the concern in his eyes. "You ready?" he asks Ruby.

She nods. "Yeah."

He crosses the room immediately, taking the suitcase from her and then heading for the hallway.

Ruby follows. She glances over when she passes me, her eyes not quite rising to meet mine. "I know it's not your fault, Cait," she says quietly. "Not… not really. But I can't stay. Not with all this. Not with what… what they did to me. What *I* did. I see it every time I close my eyes, and I just—" She shifts her shoulders like she's trying to escape something. "I have to get out of here. I'm sorry."

She flees the room. I hear the front door shut a moment later.

Panic shoots through me. No. No, she can't do this. It's too dangerous. There are people out there who'll *kill* her. Amar, Brett, the werewolves—hell, even me—we can protect her.

I take off. Ulric and Sorcha move aside quickly while I bolt toward the stairs.

"Ruby!" I race down the stairway. "Don't do this! It's not safe!"

I reach the street. The moving van is gone. Ruby is standing by the car, the door already open.

I stagger to a stop. "Ruby, please. Let me help you. Please."

She meets my eyes, one hand on the door. "Don't follow me, Cait."

Discomfort flashes over her face, but she gets into the car. I see her say something to Oliver, her eyes resolutely locked on the street ahead. He pulls the car from the curb.

Breathless on the roadside, I stare after them while they drive away.

Sorcha and Ulric follow me to Temptation. They never say a word, not when we leave my place. Not when we arrive outside the club. The topic of my near collapse at Amar's place, the topic of what happened at my apartment, *every* topic has been dropped.

I'm grateful. I don't know what to say.

I get out of my car, my body shaking, and I'm not sure if it's hunger or shock from Ruby leaving.

Just *leaving*.

A breath escapes me. I knew this was hard for her— probably not *how* hard, but still. I knew she'd been struggling.

God, I shouldn't have avoided her the past few days.

Guilt gnaws at me while I walk down the alley to the nightclub's back door. What had I been *thinking*? I should've tried harder to be there for her, my own discomfort be damned. I should've sucked it up and helped my best friend, even if she *did* look at me like I was a monster who might do something terrible to her. Because now she's gone—and with dangerous side-effect-ability things that might get her killed.

I feel sick. I can't lose her. Not now, not after everything. Not at *all*.

My fist thuds on the metal surface of the door. There has to be some way I can help her. Hire one of Ulric and Sorcha's friends to go protect her or something. I'm basically broke, yeah, but maybe—

Brett opens the door. "Hey." He glances around the alleyway. "Where's your friend?"

My stomach turns.

"The girl left," Ulric supplies.

"Oh." Brett steps aside. "All right, well, come on in."

I walk past him into the shadowy club. Like the other day, the lights are off over the dance floor, leaving the place like an abyss of darkness with only a yellow glow from the hallway and the bar at its other end to break the gloom.

"When does your club open?" Ulric asks from behind me.

"Later tonight," Brett answers. "Why?"

"Cait requires sustenance."

My sickened feeling grows worse. Not looking back, I bolt for the hallway. The short passage is dark, but it delivers me to the dimly lit bar. A few lights glow above the liquor bottles and reflect from the mirror behind them. The bar top itself glistens, obviously cleaned and prepped for tonight.

I sink onto a barstool. The thing is metal and cold, and it's been bolted to the ground to keep it from falling over. It feels incredibly stable compared to my shaking legs.

My eyes close. I'm not going to cry. Not here, where some damn incubus and a pair of werewolves will see. I'm going to be fine, and so will Ruby. So will Amar. So will everything.

Sustenance, Ulric calls it.

I swallow hard. Yeah, well, that's what it is, isn't it? Energy to keep me going—maybe even keep me alive. Who knows why I've never needed it until recently, but that's not the point. I do now.

The way my body feels like it's going to fly apart is proof of that.

And it's not a problem. I mean… it's not. Really. This isn't like Alistair—being his property and his assassin all rolled into one. This isn't like Arlene's insults, saying I'll become a slut like my mom—though, really, what the hell does that even *mean*? Like having sex, enjoying sex, is some horrible, dirty, shameful thing. It's not. So what's the big deal?

Amar flashes through my mind. His smile. His laugh. His warmth against my bare skin, and the feeling of him inside me. His smell, his taste, his *everything*. I love it all.

I love—

Desperately, I bash down the thought before it can finish. We can't be with each other, not like that. It's not possible.

I want it to be.

Oh, God help me, I desperately want it to be.

My brow furrows tightly, tears burning in my eyes. It *can't*. And *we* can't. And tonight if not sooner, I'm going to have to find some guy because of *exactly* that one fact.

I don't have a choice.

"Oh, hey."

I blink and look up, swiping the moisture from my eyes quickly. A guy is standing behind the other end of the bar, a plastic bin full of glasses in his muscular arms and an expression on his face like I've startled him with my presence. He's maybe twenty-five or so, with beige-gold skin, and he's dressed in worn jeans and a faded t-shirt that somehow still makes it entirely too easy to see how well-built he is. Waves of black hair brush his shoulders and hang to either side of his dark, short-trimmed beard and equally dark eyes.

He's hotter than hell too, and thus about the *last* thing I want to see right now.

I push away from the bar. "Sorry." I'm not even sure what I'm apologizing for. I only know I need to get out of here.

I head for the hall again.

"Are you Cait?"

I don't stop. "Yeah."

"Hey."

I glance back at him.

He sets the bin down, looking concerned. "You okay?"

I falter, not sure how to answer that. But it doesn't matter, because I really don't need to be talking to this guy right now.

He hesitates like he's trying to decide what to do, and then he walks around the side of the bar and comes toward me.

I retreat a step involuntarily.

He stops. "I'm not going to hurt you."

I shake my head, unable to explain. I need to get out of here. But it's getting harder to make myself move away. My hands are twitching with the urge to grab him.

"I'm Rafael," he offers.

Great. Now I know his name.

"You don't look so good," he continues.

A scoff leaves me. Not the greatest pickup line in history.

Like I need one?

My insides roll and I shudder, clamping my lips shut on a whimper.

"Hey." He starts toward me again.

"No." I hold up a hand, backpedaling. My legs bump into a chair.

He stops a second time. "You're hungry, aren't you?"

A string of insults present themselves, laden with desperation. Dammit, is that written across my face or something?

"And, um…" Rafael continues. "I'm guessing they didn't tell you about me?"

I look up at him in confusion.

"You can't feed on me," he says. "And you can't hurt me. It's not going to happen. But, uh…" He glances at the bar. "I could probably help you."

I eye him warily. "How?"

A brief smile flashes over his face. "Come have a seat." He nods toward the stools and then walks around the counter again, watching me as he goes.

Cautiously, I make my way back and sink unsteadily onto a barstool. Rafael turns to the array of liquor bottles.

I shake my head fast. "I don't want—"

"It's not that," he assures me. "This is just something I've made for Brett when he's ended up desperate."

My brow furrows.

He draws out a bottle from behind the others. It appears positively ordinary compared to the ones nearby; a plain, crystal box holding something that looks like water. He tugs the stopper from it and then snags a glass from underneath the bar.

Clear liquid pours into the glass. With quick, efficient motions, he twists the bottle to keep any of the contents from dripping down the sides, stops it up again, and sets it on the bar. Taking the drink in his hand, he regards it for a moment and then whispers something. I can't make out the words.

But I can see the result. Light flares, glittering and bright like a million pieces of iridescent stardust are suddenly trapped in the liquid. I gasp.

He extends it to me. I don't move.

"It's okay," he promises.

I still don't move. "What are you?"

He shrugs like I've asked a complicated question. "Someone who doesn't want to hurt you either."

My eyes go from him to the glowing liquid and back.

"Come on," he urges. "I told you, I've made this for Brett. It'll take the edge off. Trust me."

Gingerly, I take the glass. For a moment, I study its glittering contents and then cautiously raise it to my lips. Cool liquid slips into my mouth. I make myself swallow.

And it feels good.

I blink. It only takes a heartbeat before my shakiness begins to fade. My hunger too. My mind starts to clear like the liquid is washing away the craving that's been steadily trying to overwhelm me all day.

Swiftly, I gulp down the rest and then lower the glass almost reluctantly when the last drop is gone. But the fog of desperation seems to be melting from around me. My ragged breathing is gradually easing.

Rafael grins. "Better?"

I don't know what to say. I feel practically normal, whatever that is anymore. "What was that?"

He shrugs again—the same motion, like it's complicated. "Small potion. It won't last, but it'll get you through till tonight when the club opens."

Some of my elation dims. "Could I have more later?"

He hesitates. "It's not really meant for that. Too much, and there start to be… other effects. Bad ones."

I let out a breath, looking away. Of course it can't be simple. Some potion thing and my problems are gone.

"You don't want to feed on anybody?" Rafael asks.

I don't respond. I still don't know who this guy is or how he fits into this crazy demon world.

"What are you?" I ask again. "Really?"

He pauses. "Lot of things. But mostly, uh…" He grimaces. "Brett really didn't mention *anything*?"

I shake my head. I think I remember Brett and Amar talking about someone named Rafael the other day. But that's it.

He nods slowly. "All right, well. Mostly… I'm dead."

I don't move.

"A ghost," he elaborates.

I blink.

"Yeah, okay," Rafael says, a touch uncomfortably. "Well, I'm not going to hurt you, and—"

"*What?*" I choke.

He hesitates.

"You're…" I swallow hard. "You don't look—"

He chuckles. "Oh, I can ghoul it up when I want to."

I blanch.

Rafael spots my expression. "*Not* going to hurt you," he repeats firmly.

I start breathing again.

He watches me for a moment and then reaches under the counter and takes out another glass. With that same well-practiced efficiency, he fills it from a nearby spigot and then extends it to me.

I hesitate.

"Just water, I swear. You look like you could use it." A hint of his grin returns. "Or something stronger."

I take the glass. "How can you…" My hand twitches toward his. I'm not sure how to explain. "I mean, you're…"

"Holding stuff?"

I nod.

He seems to consider his words. "I've been this way for a while. Practice comes with its perks."

My gaze flicks to the plastic bin of glasses he's left on the counter. "And you used to be the bartender?"

He laughs. "I *am* the bartender."

I stare at him.

"I work with Brett," he explains. "He and I started the club together about six years ago."

My brow climbs.

Rafael shakes his head. "God, I am going to kick his ass for not explaining this." There's no rancor in his voice, just amusement.

"He started the club with a ghost."

"Oh, I wasn't dead then. That happened about four years back. Before that, I was a witch. It's sort of a prerequisite to becoming a ghost. Another perk, really." He pauses at my expression. "And you've never heard of witches like me either. Right. Damn."

I'm back to staring. I can't quite stop.

"Okay, well, a witch—*my* kind of witch—is a human who learns how to use magic. Not the same as a Touched; they're addicted to specifically what you guys give off. Witches like me learn to handle the essence of the energy that all demons use, and we do it slowly. Carefully. *Safely.* Which is how I could do that." He nods to the glass that had held the glowing liquid. "But, at the same time, magic changes us. We don't become like you. We're not demons, but we're not quite human either. And when we die, the energy we've taken in holds us here. Helps to keep us alive —minus a body, anyway."

I don't know what to say.

"It's not a bad deal, all things considered. I'm still here. I still run the bar and keep an eye on the place, same as I did before I died."

I bite back the obvious question. He seems to see it anyway.

"Kind of personal," he says.

I nod quickly. I can imagine how you *died* would be.

His lip twitches at my response. "You're taking this pretty well."

My brow knits. I don't know about that. Maybe my threshold for crazy is just topping out.

Again.

"Why don't you want to feed on anyone?" Rafael asks.

I'm still not sure I want to answer. "Kind of personal."

He pauses, studying me. I look away. I don't know how to explain—or even if I should. Who knows how anyone here would treat me if they knew the truth.

"It's not a bad thing, you know," he tries. "Being fed from. In case that, I don't know, bothers you or something."

He says it like he's not sure that's my problem. Like the idea is a little strange.

But that's not what catches me.

I look back at him, a question on the tip of my tongue.

"Brett," he acknowledges, nodding. "More than a few times, back before I died."

I blink. Rafael's lip twitches.

"Incubi and succubi are all pretty much pansexual," he explains with another shrug. "For that matter, so am I. And come on, Brett's hot."

He watches me, that grin still hovering around his lips like he's offering me the chance to join him in the expression.

I try for a smile, but my thoughts are too tangled up in what he said before. Brett, feeding from him. What that was like. I haven't really thought about this from the other side. Being a not-quite-monster who nearly killed two people has been enough to process.

"You can't make anyone do anything they don't want to," Rafael says. "The others told you that, right? Magic can't force something that isn't already there."

My skin crawls. I hadn't really thought of that either.

It definitely should have occurred to me.

I feel nauseated.

"You *heighten* the experience for humans," Rafael continues. "You make it feel amazing. But you don't force them into it. You're not like a magical roofie or something."

I can't stop myself from fidgeting.

"Is that what bothers you?" From the corner of my eye, I see him studying me like he's still trying to determine what the problem could be. "The idea that you'd be forcing someone to sleep with you?"

The scrutiny is terrible. "No." I grimace at my too-fast response. "I mean, yes. Of course. It's just—"

"What?" he asks when I cut off.

It's just I think I'm in love with Amar, I answer silently.

A pained feeling tries to claw its way up through my chest. I shift on the seat a second time, struggling to give no sign. "I don't know," I lie.

He nods, but I can tell he doesn't believe the words.

I fix my attention on anything but him. The dark wood of the bar. The way the lights glisten from its surface. And I beg whatever gods listen to demons that Rafael will drop the subject.

"Okay…" he allows after a moment. "Well, we've got a place set up for you to stay, so if you want to see that…? Maybe hang out there till the club opens and—"

I shift position all over again.

"Right," he finishes carefully. He pauses again, and then steps forward, passing straight through the bar. "Follow me?"

I stare.

He walks toward the hall.

I falter, but there isn't another option besides doing what he said. Watching him warily, I slide off the stool and start after him.

Sorcha is waiting in the shadows of the hallway, nearly invisible till I'm right on top of her. I stop, alarmed. "You—"

"Oh, she's been there the whole time," Rafael offers.

Sorcha meets the words with a flat stare. "I thought you should know—" She turns deliberately to me. "Ulric sent the man who was watching your friend after her. He'll keep an eye on her in Arizona."

A breath leaves me, almost physically painful relief pressing the air from my chest.

"We were hired to protect you both," Sorcha continues, her voice becoming ever-so-slightly gentler. "No one speci-fied that the job was to be limited by distance or location."

I choke back an incredulous laugh. I want to hug her, except she probably won't like it. "Thank you," I manage. "All of you. Thank you."

The shadows are thick, but I'd swear the hint of a smile touches her face. "It's what we were paid to do," she says, repeating Ulric's words from a day ago, though nowhere near as coldly as he'd spoken.

I nod, at a loss for how else to respond. Struggling to regroup, I glance at Rafael, who is most certainly grinning.

And I grin right back. I can't help it. I barely know this guy, but right now, I'd smile at Alistair Linden.

"So, show you the room?" Rafael offers.

I nod.

He echoes the motion. "This way."

Rafael starts off down the hall. Shaking—but this time with relief—I follow him while Sorcha trails me as silently as another ghost.

12

AMAR

He slips from the bed, and the girl doesn't stir. She won't wake for hours, he knows. The ones he feeds from never do.

In silence, he pulls on his pants and then crosses to the window. Evening light teases at the edges of the thick curtains. He pushes aside the fabric and looks down at the manor grounds three floors below. The grass is painted with gold, and long shadows stretch from the trees. Over the hills, the sun hovers on the verge of setting. The sky is a swath of pinks and yellows more vivid than any picture could capture.

He wishes Cait could see it.

A grimace twists his face. This should have been easier. He's been doing this since he was twelve, and after all the energy he'd output over the past few days, he hadn't had any choice but to feed. It shouldn't have been a problem.

Except it was.

Except he couldn't stop thinking about Cait. Her body, moving with his. Her face, overcome by what he was doing to her. Her skin, slicked with sweat and softer than silk beneath his hands. Autopilot alone had gotten him through feeding on this girl whose name he doesn't even know, but the entire time…

Damn, he wishes it'd been Cait in that bed.

His forearm braces him against the window frame. Sex has never mattered. He's never seen it the way humans do; never had the chance. It's energy he takes in because he has to. Desire has little to do with it beyond what he can elicit in others. And sure, he never wants to hurt anyone, never tries to lead anybody on, and it's in his best interest to make sure the people he's with have a good time. But ultimately, for him it's empty.

Until Cait.

His eyes close. He *misses* her. The simple act of feeding brought that home more intensely than he could have dreamed. It's hardly been more than a day since last he saw her, but for some reason, that makes no difference. This strange, alien ache inside of him has grown stronger by the hour until it's as powerful as any hunger he's ever felt. He's *craving* her, but in this way where he knows sex with her is only part of what he's longing for. In this way where it's almost *excruciating* not to know when he'll get to hold her in his arms again.

Or if she'll still be okay when he does.

His brow furrows tightly. He called Brett hours ago. He hadn't hinted he made another deal with Lucretia or that his concern was anything more than the simple practicality of avoiding a possible attack in the middle of a campus neighborhood, but he still managed to get the guy to agree to find Cait and Ruby and let them stay at Temptation. Between Brett, Rafael, the mercenaries, and all the defenses around that place, he'd done everything short of putting her and Ruby in a fortress. Lucretia wouldn't be able to double-cross him while Cait and her friend were there.

But Cait would be hungry too. She used a fair amount of energy on the guys chasing her, and she hasn't fed enough in the entire time she's known she's a Legacy. By now, she's probably starving. And he'd wanted to be there for her about that. He'd wanted to help make certain she found someone to feed from who would treat her with the care she deserved.

A breath leaves him, and with effort, he pushes the fears away. Brett might be a full-blood, and thus have the nearly nonexistent concern for others that that entailed, but he also wouldn't want trouble at his club. He'd make sure she found someone safe.

On the far side of the room, a click sounds. He pushes away from the window frame and looks toward the noise, any hint of expression disappearing from his face. The pale maid peeks past the door and then freezes when she sees him.

"Oh." Her bright red gaze darts to the girl in the bed. "Did you have enough, Master Okoro?"

"Yes, thank you. What is it?"

"Mistress Volgert would like you to know that her people are ready to leave for the nearest storage of Touched. They await your presence in the main hall whenever you are ready."

"I'll be there in a moment."

She flashes him an anxious smile and then retreats from the room, shutting the door behind her.

He sighs. It won't be much longer, he promises himself. He'll find this Touched, undo what was done to them if he can, and then leave.

It's only one job. He'll see Cait again soon.

13

My room at the club turns out to be a converted storage closet. It's only for tonight; Brett promises an actual room in his apartment upstairs once he gets some boxes moved out. But until then, I'm here, waiting. A metal shelving unit stands to my left, devoid of bottles or whatever else it might have once held. There's an old calendar on the wall, two years out of date, and the vents in the concrete ceiling rattle every time the air conditioning turns on. Brett and Rafael set up a bed in here too; a rickety, camp-style thing with a green blanket. I'm sitting on the edge of it. I don't want to think about the other reason it's here.

A knock comes at the metal door, barely audible past the music pounding through the walls. I rise and cross the two steps to the door, trying to ignore the shrink wrap that is the black dress Brett somehow found for me. It's low-cut and ends scarcely below my hips. I figure it probably belongs to Bianca.

I pull the door open. Sorcha and Ulric are on the other side.

"The club has filled sufficiently with people," Ulric states without preamble. "Your activities should go unnoticed."

I struggle to keep my nauseated reaction to the words from my face. I'm channeling Amar with everything I've got right now. His calm. His poise. The way nothing—not demons, not humans, probably not even nuclear bombs—upsets him. Because I'm going to get through this. It has to happen.

The last several hours have made that more than clear.

I walk past Ulric and Sorcha, not looking at either of them. It's the truth, really. I have to face this, and it doesn't make me a monster. I'm not going to lose control and kill someone. I don't even think that's a possibility anymore.

Because nobody is going to make me feel like Amar.

Sorcha slips past me to take the lead. I know this result wasn't what Bianca had in mind when she talked about me having sex with Amar, "getting my first time over with" or whatever. But through all these hours where I've been doing nothing but think, I've realized it's the truth. No amount of mist or magic is going to come close to what I feel when I'm with him.

I wonder if he feels the same way about me.

A sting of pain threatens to penetrate my calm, and I push the thought away fast. That's not my problem, not right now.

The thudding of the music gets louder, drowning out any hope of hearing my own thoughts, and I'm grateful. Mist hits me before I leave the hall, already emanating from the crowd of people on the gallery overlooking the dance floor. My steps balk at the sudden influx of energy, but I regroup fast. The fog takes the edge off as always, though. The trembling that's plagued me for the past several hours is already starting to fade.

I head for the stairs and the dance floor. People bump into me, brushing my arms, my sides. Mist comes with the contact, flooding me with energy. I can feel myself standing straighter. Relaxing like all my muscles are growing more limber.

The crowd is so thick that the dance floor seems to merge with the stairway and the press of bodies makes the air warm. I slip between the dancers, trying to let my mind relax like my muscles. A quick glance back confirms that Sorcha and Ulric have taken up positions at the edge of the room. Their gazes sweep the crowd, lighting on me briefly and then moving on. I turn away. They can't be my concern right now either.

I have to get this over with first.

A deep breath fills my lungs, carrying energy and mist and magic with it. I sway to the music, my attention more on the people around me than my own body. And in only a moment, I spot a guy watching me. He's tall, with brownish hair, though the color is difficult to distinguish under the dazzling, spinning lights. He comes toward me and flashes a grin when he gets close. I smile back and move nearer to him too.

His hands take my hips. He's not a bad dancer, though I'm not really a qualified judge. I've been to a club a handful of times, counting this. He could be terrible, for all I know.

But that's not really the point.

He pulls me up against him, pressing his body to mine. I haven't used any magic on him yet. I'm not sure I want to. I know what Rafael said; I can't really force anyone.

But I don't want to risk hurting him.

His hands move to my ass, and I can read the opportunism in his eyes. He's testing to see if I'll push him away.

I make myself smile instead.

He grins. His hands grip me, and the woodsy scent of his body spray surrounds me.

I wish I was with Amar.

Quickly, I turn my face away, forcing my body to keep dancing and hoping that in the dazzling blur of the lights, this guy didn't catch any change in my expression. I order myself to stay focused, and I cast a fast glance at the stairs, debating whether he'd come back with me to the storage room already or if I should give this a bit more time.

Kyle grins at me from the base of the stairway.

I gasp, freezing completely.

The crowd moves, blocking my view for only a heartbeat, and then Kyle's gone. I look around frantically, but he's nowhere to be seen. The dance floor is nothing but shadows and brief flashes of faces in the hot, swirling lights. I turn, searching for Sorcha or Ulric.

I can't find them anywhere.

"Hey!" the guy yells over the music. I glance back at him and see the confusion on his face. "What's wrong?"

I don't even know where to begin. "I—"

Someone slams into me from behind, propelling me against the guy I was dancing with. Lights flash in my eyes, and smoke alarms start blaring like the fires of hell have broken out in the middle of the dance floor.

But the sound doesn't last. The lights cut out, and so does the noise. Black and cold take the place of everything. My feet can't find the ground. Mist slices at me, frigid and lashing out like whips of ice to flay me alive. I can't even scream at the agony. The darkness seems dense. Savage, like it's fighting to keep me from leaving the club. It clogs my throat, my nose, gagging me. It fills my ears with a roar like a jet engine about to explode.

And then it's all gone. I crash to my hands and knees on concrete, and new pain shoots through my limbs at the impact. Smells of oil and gasoline hit me like a fist, and I choke.

A shrieking, gurgling sound comes from my right. I look toward it, my whole body shaking like I've received a jolt from a cattle prod.

My dance partner is on the ground. He's lying on his side, staring at me, his body curled into a fetal position. His hands have seized up into claws, and foam and spittle are frothing from his mouth. He's lurching like he's being shocked, and with every spasm, he makes that horrible noise again.

"Well, that's unpleasant."

I look up.

Kyle regards the guy briefly and then turns to me with a grin. "Hi, Cait. Nice to see you again."

The guy from the club starts thrashing and screaming. I scramble backward.

"God," Kyle comments with disgust.

Metal flashes at the corner of my eye and then a burst of sound shatters the world.

The guy lurches hard. Something wet splatters my face. He sags to the ground.

I can't breathe. Can't move.

"*Much* better."

My mouth opens, but no sound emerges. Blood is seeping from beneath the guy, staining his green t-shirt, and spreading across the concrete to encroach on his hair—

which is rust-colored, I realize, not brown like I'd thought at the club. My mistake.

I can't take my eyes from him.

"All right, then," Kyle says.

"Wha…" I don't recognize my own voice. "What—"

"Oh, he wouldn't have made it. Humans die from shadow-crossing unprotected, even without being shoved past all the defenses around that roach motel where you were hiding." He chuckles. "So how ya been, Cait?"

I want to scream.

Kyle sighs. "Get her up, would you? This is pathetic."

Hands grab me and haul me upright. My wide eyes manage to turn from the guy on the ground to the man holding my arm in a vice-like grip. He's got to weigh three hundred pounds, and he's easily a foot taller than I am, with a snake tattooed in strangely metallic ink on his neck. Other people surround us, a dozen at least. They regard me expressionlessly while one of them tucks a gun away beneath his jacket.

I look back toward Kyle. He's still grinning like this is some great joke.

Reality is creeping back, though. Awareness of my body and the space around me. And with it comes rage. Cold, burning rage.

"What do you want?" I growl.

"Oh, look at that. She's being brave now." He smirks. "We want your help, Cait. Don't you remember?"

"I don't work for fucking *Linden*. Get that through your head, asshole."

Kyle makes a dismissive gesture. "Yeah, yeah, we figured that out. But that doesn't change much for Josephine's little girl, now does it?"

My stomach turns to lead. I fight to keep from showing any sign.

"Quite the revelation about your demon ancestry, isn't it? Too bad I never met your mom. You and I could have had this discussion ages ago and saved a lot of trouble."

"What do you want?" I repeat, my voice tightly controlled.

"To find somebody. A Touched who… well, let's just say they're different than the rest. Special, sort of like you."

"Go screw yourself."

He laughs.

"You tell your boss, Lucretia, she can shove it too. I'm not—"

"I'll be sure to do that," he assures me dryly. "But here's the thing, Cait… I don't work for Volgert."

I freeze.

"Well," he hedges. "*Technically* I do, and up until a certain Legacy asshole started making deals and fucking up my plans to be the incubi in *charge* of finding that Touched —and thus the one in *control* of them—I was happy to keep everyone believing that. But then, that's the point with coups. They look like one thing when they're actually not." His brow twitches up. "Sort of like your friend Amar."

I stop breathing.

"See, I may not know exactly what he can do, but that doesn't really bother me, because I *do* know he's made another bargain with that nostalgic old relic, Lucretia, all for the soppy little reason of keeping you safe. Hell, he's even given up his independence to seal the deal for your protection. And now he's gotten himself into a *terribly* vulnerable position and he doesn't have a clue." His grin returns. "Be a shame if something happened as a result."

Kyle chuckles when I don't respond. "Here's how it's going to go: you find the Touched. You help my people bring them back to me. And you don't tell anyone about it, or you get to watch me kill Amar and feed his body to a wood chipper. How's that sound?"

Quivers start in my belly, radiating up through my chest.

A satisfied smile twists Kyle's face. "You suck as a demon, you know. Human as hell. And him… damn, I would've expected better. Guess he's not the paragon of a Legacy that he pretends to be."

"You—" My eyes flash around, skipping across the parking garage where we're standing. A yellow door to my right bears a sign about stairs. A large exit ramp of broken concrete stretches ahead of me, leading who knows where. "People will be looking for me. You can't just—"

"Who? Those furry wastes of space you called body-guards? Yeah, we took care of them. You're on your own, Cait."

My shivers get stronger. I can't believe him. I don't *want* to believe him. I hardly know Sorcha and Ulric but I… dammit, I like them.

The snake-tattooed monster holding my upper arm gives a small snort.

My gaze snaps to him. Static shoots over my body before I even register the impulse.

He grunts. A shimmer ripples through his skin, bright and metallic like the human color of his flesh is only an illusion. He glances down at me, and for a moment, his eyes are orbs of steel.

"Ow," he growls, more anger than pain in his tone.

I wince when his grip clenches harder on my bicep.

"Clock's ticking, Cait," Kyle says. "You run, you fight, Amar dies. So what's it going to be?"

I look back to him. I can't do this. I won't. But after what happened to Ruby, I don't doubt for a second that this bastard will try to hurt Amar.

I don't even trust that Kyle won't hurt him regardless of what I say.

He grins like he can see what I'm thinking. "Human as *hell*," he repeats. "You take one step out this door without me, and I'll have your boyfriend dead faster than you can say—"

All the shadows seem to shift at once, and suddenly, Katsuro and two dozen others are there. The yellow door to the stairwell bursts from its hinges and Ram barrels through the opening, the guy called Tank and three other enormous people on his heels.

"No!" Kyle rages.

One of Kyle's people rushes toward Katsuro. It's a mistake. Katsuro moves so fast, the air seems to blur around him, and suddenly, the other man is on the ground at Katsuro's back with blood pouring from a gaping wound at his neck. With barely a pause, Katsuro swipes the blood from his hand and then turns, his pitch-black eyes radiating a threat to all the others in front of him. Motioning quickly, the vampire directs his people toward the guy holding me.

Fury snarls across Kyle's face. He lunges for me. I try to retreat, but the monster holding me is too strong.

Another one of Katsuro's people gets there first, slamming into Kyle and sending him flying.

Air ripples around Kyle. He rolls in midair and lands in a cloud of dust without any evidence of injury. He throws a hand out and lightning arcs from his fingertips, striking the guy who attacked him. The demon falls.

"Get the girl!" Kyle shouts. "Don't let them take her!"

Several more of Katsuro's people race at him. Kyle scans them fast, and his conclusion is clear. He bolts across a thin line of shadow on the ground and disappears.

The rest of his people rush at me.

Katsuro's people intercept them. Screams break out. I gasp, trying to look away as blood hits the walls.

The guy holding me has other plans.

Wrenching me around, he starts for the rear of the parking garage and another bright yellow door I can see in the distance there. I try to slow him, digging my heels into the rough concrete, stumbling to keep from being dragged when that doesn't work. My hand claws at his fingers on my arm.

I'd stand a better chance of breaking steel.

Tank and Ram race past us and circle fast, blocking our path. The snake-tattooed guy skids to a stop, yanking me to his side. He's bigger than the two of them, I realize. Slower, maybe, but so huge that I'm suddenly afraid for the two trolls.

Ram doesn't seem to care. He grins, his metal teeth glinting in the light. "Drop her or die."

A growl rumbles from the tattooed man. He hauls me around, keeping me between him and Ram. I choke on the pain of my muscles grinding against my bones.

"All right," Ram says.

He charges toward me.

The tattooed guy roars. His grip shifts, and suddenly, I'm flying, my whole body hurled sideways.

Someone snags me before I hit the ground. For a heart-beat, I stare at the concrete only inches from my face, a scream trapped in my throat. Quivering with shock, I manage to twist my head to the side and look back at the person holding me.

Katsuro smiles, sharp fangs edging over his lip. "Hello, Cait."

Electricity crackles through the air and slams into a nearby wall in a shower of sparks and ballistic concrete. My eyes snap over. Ram and Tank have the other troll. He doesn't look like he'll get up again. But several of Kyle's people are racing toward us. Magic crackles around them.

And then Katsuro is moving again. In a swift motion, he lifts me and sets me upright. "Time to go."

He pulls me backward, and the world vanishes into a blur of shadows.

14

Everything returns in a rush. The mist and darkness give way to an alley beside a busy street, and the sound of a horn honking startles me, as does the laughter that follows. I can't see what caused it all. My gaze darts around, landing on the worn bricks on either side of me and the narrow view of a brightly lit storefront across the street, but I don't recognize anything from this angle. We aren't near Temptation, I can tell. But I'm not sure where we are.

"This way." Katsuro pulls me toward a metal door tucked deeper in the shadows of the alleyway.

I plant my feet, stopping our advance. "What—where are we?"

"Close to safety, but not there yet."

I cast another glance toward the road. The shadows are sharp here, I notice, drawn in sheer lines by the sides of the building and the bright street lamps. Funny how that simple fact seems so threatening.

But this isn't good either. Yeah, Katsuro and his people

basically saved my life, but that doesn't mean they're not a danger to me too. They seem determined to make use of whatever it is I can theoretically do, same as Kyle.

And for pretty much the same reason.

Katsuro looks back when he realizes I haven't followed. "Those demons could still find us here. We must get out of sight."

"I need to get in touch with Amar."

Even if I have no idea how to do that.

I push the thought aside. I do know where to find Brett, and that'll be enough. "Kyle threatened to kill Amar if I refused to do what he wanted. He said Amar was in danger and didn't even know it." I can see the unwillingness in Katsuro's expression. "Please, I have to get back to Temptation and warn—"

"Has he told you what he is?" Katsuro cuts in.

I falter. "What?"

"Amar. Has he told you?"

I stare at him while my mind flashes back to Kyle, to Ram, to everyone who keeps hinting at Amar being some horrible thing. But *unlike* everybody else, there's no contempt or alarm in Katsuro's eyes. There's only an intensity like the question is a matter of life or death.

And before I can even speak, he seems to read the answer on my face.

"Do you *trust* either of them, then?" Katsuro presses.

"Trust either of—"

"Do you believe this Kyle person will do as he says or that Amar is trustworthy?"

Chills creep over me. He thinks I can tell what's true with this power everyone says I have. But it doesn't matter. About this one thing, at least, I know I'm right, regardless. "Yes." I nod. "On both counts, yes."

Katsuro grimaces. "Very well." He strides past me to the line of shadow on the concrete. "Are you familiar with what is necessary for shadow-crossing on your own?"

I hesitate and then shake my head. Without a word, he extends a hand to me. Gingerly, I wrap my fingers around his, working not to react to how cool and inhuman they feel. We step forward. The alley disappears.

Sirens are the first thing I hear when we return to the normal world. Quickly, I jog to the exit of this new alley and peek around the corner.

Flashing lights nearly blind me. Down the street from us, cop cars and three ambulances surround the front entrance to Temptation, clearing space like they're trying to keep everyone away. A crowd has formed beyond official-looking barricades, but in the glare, I can't make out any faces I recognize.

Which doesn't mean much. God, I hope Kyle hasn't come back here as well.

"The humans believe it was a bomb." Katsuro stops beside me. "The demons shredded through thick layers of defense to take you out of there as they did. The backlash was intense. Several of their number were killed."

"How do you—"

"I had agents there as well. They reported the situation to me the moment you were taken."

I stare at him, but he doesn't look my way, his gaze fixed on the crowds like he's searching for someone. "Who *are* you?"

He doesn't take his focus from the road. "That remains a rather complicated question."

"Are you with those Guardians?"

That pulls his attention to me. I can see the surprise in his dark eyes.

"Those people who attacked us at the salvage yard. They said they—"

The surprise dies into something cold. "We are *not* with them."

He goes back to studying the crowd.

A breath leaves me. Okay… fine. That's not really an answer, but truth is, I don't have time for this anyway. I need to find Brett and figure out from him how to reach Amar.

I'm not the only one in danger tonight—and I trust Amar more than anyone else right now.

I glance at the road. There's a gap between the barricades near the alley that leads to the rear entrance of the club. I don't see any cops near it. Not many bystanders either.

I dart across the street.

"Cait!" Katsuro hisses.

I don't look back. I duck into the shadows and keep moving. The rear door is closed, and when I try the handle, it turns out to be locked as well.

My debate about what to do lasts only a heartbeat. I knock as hard as I can. Even if there are cops inside, maybe I can explain. Say I'm looking for Brett or Rafael or something. My eyes flick back to the street while I wait. Katsuro is striding after me, but no one else seems to be looking my way. Over the wail of more sirens approaching, my actions seem to have gone unnoticed by anyone on the street.

The door opens. Rafael peers out and then freezes when he sees me. Alarm rushes across his face. "Cait! Shit, are you—" He catches sight of Katsuro coming up behind me, and he tenses. "Who's this?"

Katsuro twitches his head in a brief nod. "Hisakawa Katsuro."

"He helped me," I add quickly.

Rafael eyes him warily. "All right." He looks back to me like he's still in shock.

"May we enter?" Katsuro presses.

"Uh, yeah." Rafael regroups fast. "But the cops will be coming inside any moment now. I've got some obfuscation spells going, which should buy us some time to secure this place before the bomb squad arrives, but you—"

He looks over and moves away sharply when someone strides up to his side.

"What happened?" Sorcha demands. "Are you all right?"

I stare. She's injured. There's a rip in her jacket only a few inches from her heart. Dried blood crusts the leather. I can see darker stains on her shirt. "Are you?" I blurt.

Sorcha grimaces. "Get inside."

I hurry into the club.

Katsuro moves to follow me, but Sorcha steps into his path. A low growl leaves her.

"I mean no harm," Katsuro says.

"Did you send demons into this place?" Sorcha replies, her tone barbed.

Katsuro seems to weigh his words carefully. "Two vampires and a troll, yes. I ordered them to watch her, for protection only." He leans his head carefully toward me, not breaking eye contact with Sorcha. "They were not associated with the ones who assaulted this place."

She's silent for a heartbeat. "You should go to them."

He pauses a second time. "They are no longer here, and I am not leaving Cait."

The hairs on my arms stand on end, and I don't even know why. It's like suddenly the ground beneath us all has become the edge of a cliff, and I can just picture the bloody death that waits if we fall over the side. "He helped—"

"I heard you." Sorcha doesn't take her eyes from him. A moment creeps by, and then she steps aside, her every motion guarded.

Katsuro nods once and then walks past her, his movements as cautious as hers had been. "Thank you."

I can't tell if he's speaking to her or me.

Watching them both warily, Rafael shuts the door.

"This way," Sorcha says to me.

I don't move. "Where's Ulric?"

She hesitates and my stomach drops. I try to brace myself for the answer. "Alive, last I saw, but his injuries are more severe than mine. Other members of our pack have arrived; they are with him."

I can't stop my gaze from twitching to the tear in her coat again and the edge of the bloodstains I can see beneath. "What hap—"

"The obfuscation spell is only temporary," Sorcha interrupts. "It would be best to get you out of sight quickly."

"Agreed," Katsuro states.

She treats him to a cold stare that lasts a heartbeat longer than remotely comfortable and then motions for me to precede her. "We must find you a more secure location. Your room will suffice for the moment, but it would be best to leave this place—"

"No." I shake my head fast. "I have to call Amar first."

Her jaw tightens.

I glance at Rafael. "Do you have his number?"

He hesitates. "Yeah, but—"

"Why do you need to call Amar?" Bianca strides out of the hallway toward us.

I hesitate, thrown by her presence. Some part of me just

wants to ignore her, though I know it's childish and won't get me anywhere besides. "Because he's in danger."

"Why?"

My muscles bunch at her accusatory tone. "What are you doing here?" I ask instead.

"A bunch of assholes just attacked my brother's club, all for the sake of getting to you. I came to make sure Brett wasn't dead. Now why do you need to call Amar?"

I grit my teeth. "Because the asshole in charge threatened to *kill* Amar if I didn't help him get what he wanted. And now I'm here, which means he might make good on the threat." I look back at Rafael. "Number?"

He glances at Bianca rather than answer. The girl is already reaching for her cell. She swipes through the screens like their delay annoys her almost as much as I do, and then she lifts the phone to her ear.

"Amar, it's Bianca. Some jackasses did a fucking blitz attack on Temptation, and Cait heard they're after you next. Watch your back and call me when you get this."

She hangs up and then turns to Rafael like nothing happened. "Brett wanted to know about those extra defenses you were going to put in place."

"They're up."

"Good."

I look between them. "Is that it? Don't you know where he is or—"

"Amar's a big boy," Bianca interrupts. "He can take care of himself."

I stare at her.

"So, uh—" Rafael starts to me. "Your room is safe. I've got those same defenses around it. So if you want to get cleaned up before you all move somewhere else…"

My brow furrows. Cleaned up? Why the hell would he think I—

"The blood, Cait," he elaborates uncomfortably, as if he can see my confusion. "You're covered in blood."

I look down for the first time and choke. My arms are speckled with red. Above the ridiculous dress, my chest is too. The guy, I realize. When they shot him.

My knees want to buckle. I freeze, fighting not to fall apart in front of nearly everyone I know in the demon world.

"Restroom's this way," Bianca snaps.

She jerks her head toward the hall.

Somehow, I make my legs move. Make them hold me upright. I start toward the hallway and then pause when Bianca marches ahead of me and shoves open the restroom door.

"Come on," she orders.

"I-I don't—"

"Go."

I watch her for a heartbeat, weighing whether smacking her would *possibly* go well. The anger helps, though. I stride past her on legs that are far steadier than a moment ago.

She follows me inside and snags a handful of paper towels from the dispenser. With a quick motion, she twists the handles on one of the sinks. Water gushes from the faucet.

I balk. "I can—"

"Yeah, or you could pass out. Don't think I didn't see that reaction out there. Just get over here."

I hear the door behind me and glance back to find Sorcha slipping into the room as well. For some reason, the sight is reassuring. Like, maybe Sorcha will keep me from punching this bitch.

Or maybe she'll help.

I let out a breath, feeling a bit hysterical with anger and adrenaline. Working to stay calm, I grab my own handful of paper towels and then walk to the sink.

Bianca scoffs.

I ignore the sound and dunk the paper towels beneath the faucet. Warm water soaks into the brown material. With meticulous focus, I begin swiping my forearms.

The blood smears, and my stomach turns. His blood. The guy from the dance floor. I'd never even asked his name.

I close my eyes briefly, trying to concentrate. The speckles are larger on my shoulders. A few have formed drips, now dried. Swallowing hard, I rub at them. The residue turns my skin red.

I wonder when someone will find his body.

My hand shakes. I suck down a steadying breath, but I can't make my hand move to keep washing the blood away. The paper towel is starting to become too saturated, though. I probably need another one. Setting it down, I reach toward the dispenser.

I catch sight of myself in the mirror and stop. Blood is splattered across my face, making me look as if I belong in a horror movie. Bits of my hair are stuck together, like there's blood dried in the dark strands too. Oh my God.

Bianca grabs my shoulder. "For pity's sake, just—"

I yank away and stumble a few steps back. "Don't touch me."

She stares at me.

I can't speak. I feel like a scream is trapped inside my chest, strong enough that, any moment now, it's going to explode out and tear my whole body apart. And all I can do is shake with the force of it. The silent, terrible force of my horror at watching that guy die.

Because of me.

"Cait." Bianca starts toward me again.

"Don't!" I scream.

A pulse of energy leaves me. Bianca stumbles back while every mirror in the room shatters.

I freeze. Bianca looks over at me, fury clear on her face, and then her gaze goes beyond me to Sorcha.

Panicked, I turn. She's okay. Her amber eyes are strangely brighter than before, nearly glowing, and there's something wild in her gaze. But she's not dead. I didn't kill her too.

My gorge rises.

"Get out," Bianca orders.

I glance back.

She's looking to Sorcha. "Now."

The brightness in Sorcha's eyes dims back toward something more human. She glances between us warily.

I shake my head fast. "No, you don't—"

"I said *now*," Bianca repeats, an edge to her voice.

Sorcha looks at me. "I can hear everything from outside the door," she says as if she's trying to reassure me.

She slips out of the room. Bianca releases a breath like she's been holding it.

"You are going to *kill* somebody, goddammit," she hisses. "Get a grip."

My body shudders so hard, I think I might fly apart. I squeeze my eyes closed as if that can keep me together. I *already* killed somebody. Some poor guy whose name I didn't even know, now lying on a parking garage floor with his blood and body growing cold on the concrete, all because he wanted to dance with me—

"Shit," Bianca mutters.

Trembling, I open my eyes.

"Sorry," she says.

I stare at her.

"Whatever happened out there," she continues. "I'm sure it wasn't your fault."

She says the words like she isn't actually certain she believes them. But like, at the same time, she might.

I eye her distrustfully. "Why are you helping me?"

"What?"

"Why are you helping me? This. Ruby. You hired some of the mercenaries, too. Brett and Amar told me. But—"

She looks at me like I've asked her something offensive.

I struggle onward. "You pretty much seem like you hate me most of the time, so why—"

She makes an irritated noise. "God, you're so human."

I slam my hand down onto the edge of the sink. Bianca tenses like she's bracing herself for another onslaught of magic.

And I don't know what to say. I'm sick of this. Of demons. Of being *insulted*, just because I'm not soulless like so many of them. I know what Amar has said about her, how well he thinks of her. But maybe Amar is wrong.

Maybe in her own way, she's no better than Kyle.

I head for the door.

"You're going to hurt him."

I stop and look back. She hasn't moved any closer. Her brow twitches up, icy certainty in her eyes.

My head shakes. "I wouldn't—"

"You'll *get* him hurt. You think I haven't seen how you're fucking with his head? Amar was *safe* before now.

Safe from the Houses, from Lucretia, and *damn* well safe from—" She cuts off sharply and grimaces like she's revising what she'd been about to say. "I know you think *we're* the screwed-up ones, not letting ourselves be manipulated by every hormonal bit of nonsense humans adore. That maybe he's broken or some bullshit like that. But we're not. *He's* not. We're stronger than you. But what you're doing is putting his life at risk in more ways than you can *possibly* understand. The lives of everyone else I know too, for that matter."

"So why are you helping me?"

She hesitates. "Because I promised Amar I would."

Incredulity spreads through me. She promised him. Just… promised him. She treated me to a whole demon tirade… and that's *it?*

She looks away. "I'm keeping him safe."

I'm not even certain what to say. "Why do you care if Amar is safe?"

Her jaw works around. "Because I made him a promise."

My brow furrows. Her tone is strange. There's more to those words than before. Like, history. Loads of it. "When?"

She looks at me sharply, and for a heartbeat, she doesn't do anything but stare. "You think you *know* something about me?"

I blink.

She strides toward me. "You think you're *reading something?* I heard about you. Who they think you are. Rumor travels fast around here, and I will *not* have you—"

"I'm not!" I back away quickly and bump into a stall.

The door to the restroom opens. Sorcha looks in.

Bianca doesn't spare her a glance, stopping only inches

from me. "When we were thirteen years old, Amar saved my life when no other demon would. So I returned the favor and saved his. Happy?"

I glance at Sorcha. Cautiously, the woman retreats. The door closes. "What happened?" I ask softly.

Bianca eyes me up and down. "House bullshit. A dozen assholes from Linden had me cornered. My father was elsewhere, and Brett was too, and the sonofabitch bodyguards Dad hired took a bribe to let them do whatever they wanted to me. No one should've stepped in—it wasn't their problem—but Amar did. He stopped them."

"Alone?"

She's silent for a moment. "Yeah."

I gape at her, a question on the tip of my tongue. There's more to it. Obviously, there has to be. And I can hear that fact in her voice.

She doesn't elaborate, though. "I had my head down. He didn't explain. But a while after that, his father died, and Amar needed help too. I promised to give that to him." She meets my gaze, a chilling intensity to her blue eyes. "I keep my promises."

I nod carefully, not sure what other response to offer.

Bianca steps away from me. I let out a breath slowly.

"Finish getting cleaned up," she orders, striding back to the sink. She grabs a handful of paper towels from the dispenser and then extends them to me.

Warily, I cross the small space and take the towels from her. Turning on the faucet, I dunk them beneath the water and then start wiping my face, still watching her from the corner of my eye.

"You have enough energy left in you to keep going?" she asks when I'm done.

I give a small shrug, keeping my eyes from twitching to the shattered mirrors beside me. "Maybe."

"Fine. Then whenever we get to someplace where you *won't* destroy things connected to my family, we'll work on getting that magic of yours under control."

I hesitate. "Okay. Thanks."

Bianca doesn't respond, but simply walks toward the door.

I watch her go, residual shivers crawling through my skin because suddenly it clicks, that look I'd seen in her eyes only moments before. She would have killed me. She's not like Brett—laid-back and generally unconcerned with anyone around him. She's not like Kyle, who's cruel for fun.

She's like Sorcha. Like Ulric. A wolf, but without even a *shred* of their humanity.

Bianca wouldn't have hesitated to see me dead, back at the first sign that I was becoming a threat to her or anyone who matters to her. But she hadn't, and the weird thing is that now, I'm fairly certain she never will. I'm in the camp of people she'll help, and for one reason and one reason alone.

She promised Amar.

"You coming?" she snaps.

"Yeah."

I drop the paper towels into the garbage, studiously avoiding my own reflection in the shattered mirrors, and I follow her out the door.

15

AMAR

Even in the shadows and the moonlight, the house isn't much to look at from the outside. A crumbling wreck with a roof so overgrown by moss that it looks like an intentional design feature. The porch is likewise falling apart, and he wouldn't put money on anyone being able to walk across it safely. Nothing but trees surrounds the building. Whatever road may once have existed has been swallowed by grass and underbrush.

His gaze slides to the forest. It'd taken them a small eternity to reach this abandoned hovel, miles from civilization, and now he isn't certain how far he'd have to go to find the nearest house or sign of life. He hasn't seen so much as an electrical pole for the past hour, and even his cell phone has long since lost its connection to the outside world. If Linden wanted a place to hide this unusual Touched, this would be it.

Instinct borne of nearly a decade among demons stirs in him. His focus slides to the side, and a moment later, the undergrowth quivers and one of Lucretia's agents appears.

The man's skin looks ashen next to his camo gear, a fact that doesn't distinguish him from any of the other vampires Lucretia sent along. Amar never bothered to ask the names of the people with him. It isn't important. Nothing is, beyond getting this over with.

Swiftly, the guy motions. Leaves whisper against one another when his companions slip from the bushes, moving to surround the house.

The guy looks at him expectantly. He ignores the glance but starts toward the house as well, circling toward the cellar access on the side of the building. The basement would be the best place for the chains and cages the Houses use to keep their victims under control.

In silence, the vampire moves ahead of him, aiming for the same destination. Several of the others do as well.

A simple brass lock secures the latch. From a pouch on his belt, the vampire draws out a small crystal and sweeps it quickly above the cellar door. The wooden surface seems to ripple, like it's coated in the faintest of sheens from an oil slick. Straightening again, the vampire tucks the stone away and then draws out another tool. The witch-cursed troll bone clunks onto the door. The oil-slick ripples become agitated for a moment and then disappear.

Amar's eyes narrow. That was too easy.

The vampire doesn't seem to agree. Returning the bone to his belt, he tosses a quick glance at his companions and then snaps the lock away. With both hands, he yanks the cellar door wide.

Nothing moves. The stairway appears empty.

The others start forward warily, testing the steps before trusting any weight to them. Amar follows them into the black. His kind don't consistently have the excellent night vision of the vampires or werewolves. Instead, their eyesight varies, with some among the incubi and succubi able to see better in the darkness than others.

After all these years, he's learned he's among the best.

They reach the bottom of the steps. His eyes dart across the space, picking out the shapes of bolts on the walls. Chains dangle from them, thick and heavy as if meant to restrain rabid beasts. There are no cages and, more importantly, no Touched.

But there is a television. A flat panel affixed high on the wall. Small cameras hang near it, their tiny red lights blinking.

The leader among Lucretia's people throws a disgusted look around. "Dammit, they—"

On the far side of the cellar, the door to the house opens. Boots clunk on the stairway. Noise comes from behind him. He turns to see more people hurrying down the steps from the outside.

And they have guns, knives, all of them almost certainly witch-cursed. He tenses while Lucretia's people draw their weapons as well.

The television flares to life, casting the whole room in its glow. "Well," comes a cultured voice. "This *is* a surprise."

Amar's gaze snaps to the screen.

Alistair Linden smiles at them from what appears to be a luxuriously decorated lounge. He's dressed in a suit and seated in a wingback leather chair, flames crackling in the fireplace beside him. Holding a glass of liquor in his hand, he regards the camera like he's been caught in a pleasant moment of relaxation.

"What is this?" the vampire demands.

"What does it look like?" Alistair chuckles. "We have a psychic in our possession, silly boy. She saw you coming.

Though I must say, she hadn't mentioned *you* would be here, Mister Okoro. Again you appear where I do not expect you. This is becoming a rather disappointing habit of yours."

Alistair's people adjust their grips on their weapons. Lucretia's people immediately do the same.

"Oh, careful now," Alistair admonishes from the screen. "No need for that."

His people hesitate like the words are unexpected.

"I'd say plans have changed now, haven't they, Mister Okoro? But what she's said about this evening… oh, that is starting to make much more sense." A hint of a smile pulls at Alistair's lip while he regards the screen. "How intriguing." He draws a breath, shifting a bit in his chair. "Fall back, all of you. Leave them be."

A heartbeat of a pause follows, and then Alistair's people edge toward the stairs.

"I'd recommend staying out of my way once you've finished up here, my boy. What comes next for Volgert needn't be your concern. Consider that a fair warning. And as for Cait…" Alistair shakes his head. "I know you believe she could be advantageous to you, what with her heritage and all. I won't deny your strategy is sound. But you should let her join me. There is more to her than meets the eye, Mister Okoro, and what's been hinted, what's been *seen*…" He makes a worried noise. "It's not too late, you know, for either of you. Safety is still yours for the taking, just as it's always been. All you have to do is ask. Think on that—for both your sakes." He lifts his glass slightly and tilts it toward the camera. "Good evening, Mister Okoro."

The screen turns black. The doors shut as Alistair's people leave the basement behind.

And then only Lucretia's people remain.

The leader reaches for his walkie-talkie. "Report."

A moment creeps past in silence, and then the speaker on the radio crackles. "Hostiles leaving the area."

Relief crosses the vampire's face.

A crackle comes from the walkie-talkie again. "Contact from Operations, sir. Response negative. I repeat, response negative. Target acquisition failed."

Watching the vampire, Amar doesn't show his confusion at the words. Response? Target acquisition? He glances at the others. Alistair had known something. Had been *implying* something, and there aren't many good versions of what that could be.

His attention returns to the leader, who has become utterly motionless.

And that, more than anything, sends every alarm in his body clamoring to life.

"Understood," the man replies.

The vampire puts the radio away and then glances at the others. With the speed of their kind, every one of them suddenly turns, aiming their weapons. The leader gets off a shot.

The rest aren't fast enough.

Amar's world goes still. Frozen for a heartbeat that lasts all of eternity, and in it, there's only silence. Pain like a distant flash grazes across his bicep, but it's nothing compared to the power flooding his veins. The darkness of black holes, of the hearts of dead worlds floating forever alone in the emptiness of space, the magic roars through his body, cataclysmic and yet totally in his control. In an instant, the void surges up and lashes across the room in an invisible wave that he hates beyond words. He wishes with everything he has that he wasn't this. *Like* this. But then, this is what continues, time and again, to save his life.

Every demon around him collapses to the floor.

A breath leaves him, and a small shudder runs through his body, for all that the expenditure of magic barely tapped the reserves of energy he has inside. He's one of the strongest incubi in existence—another gift from his father, and another fact that, like this horror-show talent he inherited, continues to keep him free and alive.

But that doesn't mean using the ability is ever a welcome experience.

He glances around, despite the fact he knows what he'll see. The vampires are dead—truly dead, beyond even what their kind can recover from. Like toppled dolls, they lie on the ground with their limbs askew, though from the lack of wounds, one could almost think they were asleep. But their eyes tell a different story. Wide with terror, their unseeing gazes stare emptily at the ceiling, at the walls, at him.

He turns away, silently hoping their faces won't join those already in his nightmares. The vampires must have suspected what they would be up against the moment they turned their weapons on him.

The question is why they chose to do it in the first place.

His gaze goes to the stairway behind him and the door to the outside at its top. Operations. There's only one person that would be. But for Lucretia to send him all this way only to have her people turn on him—

Target acquisition failed.

His blood turns cold. Cait.

He bolts up the stairs.

Cait will be fine.

He hangs onto the thought while he speeds down the rough dirt track. It took forever to reach the hollow in the forest where Lucretia's people had hidden their cars, and longer still to clear away the branches covering one of the vehicles. The keys had been where the vampires left them, tucked into the console and not in a pocket where they might have made noise at the wrong moment. Likewise, none of the other forces Lucretia sent along—the ones who kept watch outside while he and the vampires went into the house—attempted to come near him or slow him down. They had to know it would have cost them their lives.

And it doesn't matter anyway, because *Cait is fine*.

He digs his phone from his pocket, and then grimaces when the motion causes a twinge of pain to emanate from the hastily wrapped bullet graze on his arm. But the trunk of the car had turned up a small first-aid kit and bandages, and the wound isn't bad anyway. It'll be barely noticeable in a day or so.

Lifting the phone, he takes his eyes from the road to glance at the screen briefly. Relief hits him when a bar of signal appears. The feeling is short-lived, however, because a second later, a voicemail notification arrives.

Bracing himself, he touches the icon and then lifts the cell to his ear.

"Amar, it's Bianca. Some jackasses did a fucking blitz attack on Temptation, and Cait heard they're after you next. Watch your back and call me when you get this."

He lowers the phone. *Cait* heard… He draws a breath. Then she's there, *still* there, and not hurt or dead.

His foot eases off the gas pedal. The car slows to a more rational speed. For a moment, he doesn't do anything but drive, waiting till he is certain his voice won't give anything away.

He touches another icon and then lifts the phone again.

"Hello?" Bianca answers.

"It's me. Got your message. Already taken care of."

Bianca pauses. He's never gone into detail of what he can do, and she's never exactly asked. It's an unspoken understanding between them, the fact they both have their secrets. He knows she suspects, though. Whispers of what his father could do, gleaned over the years by Chastain family spies, meant it wasn't too much of a leap for her to guess he inherited those "gifts" too.

"Good," she replies shortly. "Well, Cait's with me at Temptation. Cops believe they're going to lock the club down—the morons. We'll have the place to ourselves soon as they go. You coming this way?"

He hesitates. He wants to answer yes. After all, returning to Temptation had been the plan.

But he knows Cait still isn't fully safe.

What's been hinted… what's been seen…

He shoves the memory of Alistair's words aside. One thing at a time. "I have something to do first."

"All right. Take care of yourself."

His lip twitches. From Bianca, that's practically emotional. "Yeah."

He hangs up and sets the phone aside. He wishes he could have found a way to speak to Cait, but there wasn't any reason Bianca would believe. No message she couldn't simply pass along.

And he's not sure how it would have affected him, hearing Cait's voice.

Air leaves him. He needs to stay focused. They aren't out of danger yet.

The hours of driving pass in a blur, lost to his silent debate of how best to handle the situation. Lucretia will know the moment he shows up on her doorstep that her plan failed. Chances are, she *already* knows, considering her people were likely meant to check in after their task was complete.

There's no telling what she might have waiting for him.

He slows the car several miles shy of the manor. He's close enough now for shadow-crossing, but he's not certain he should try it. The defenses on her property are bound to be formidable.

But aiming for somewhere outside the building will probably work, and regardless, it's safer than driving. Or at least faster. If he needs to make a quick retreat, the pain of passing those barriers will be significantly less of an issue than being shot while he tries to drive away.

He stops the car and gets out. He'll give her a chance to talk, he decides. See how she can explain sending her people after him—just in case he gets the impression there are others out there still waiting for their chance to attack. Better to be prepared because, next time, Cait might not be so lucky and he might not have warning enough to stop them.

His eyes close briefly. He allows himself a moment to make sure he's calm and focused, and then he heads away from the car. A nearby tree provides enough contrast between the moonlight and the pavement to give him somewhere to cross, and then the road is gone and the manor lies before him.

For a moment, nothing stirs. Even the breeze has lulled.

The front door opens, and the petite maid appears. "Master Okoro?"

She sounds surprised to see him. Her gaze darts around the moonlit driveway, obviously noticing the lack of a vehicle. He ignores her, glancing across the windows and the rooftops, searching for threats.

The manor appears utterly still.

"Are you all right?" She starts down the steps toward him.

"Don't," he warns.

She stops, alarmed.

"Where is Lucretia?"

The girl appears perturbed. "T-the Mistress is upstairs. Is everything all right?"

"Tell her I wish to speak to her. Now."

Blinking fast, the maid falters. She retreats toward the manor, never quite looking away from him.

He waits. Somewhere in the distance, a coyote howls. Crickets, still hanging on despite the autumn cold, resume chirping in the silver-touched grass.

And nothing else changes. The manor could be empty for how quiet it seems.

The front door opens again. The maid peeks out. "This way, sir?" She motions for him to come inside.

He walks to the door, the dark and cold power coursing beneath his skin like a storm waiting to engulf the world. Lucretia might have a backup plan to kill him, he knows, and it might even work.

But it would be a plan no one in this building will probably survive.

Anxiety clear in her scurrying speed, the girl leads him upstairs and down the hall. By the end of the corridor, two men stand like butlers. They push a door wide for him as he approaches. The girl falls back, avoiding his eyes when he walks past.

Lucretia waits by the small, round table in the center of the room. Red roses fill a vase beside her, and candles glow from the chandelier overhead. It could feel like a reenactment of their conversation this morning, if not for the tension he can see in her face.

The magic beneath his skin grows stronger.

"Hello, Amar," Lucretia says politely, a tight compression of her lips making some pretense at being a smile.

He wastes no time with preamble. "Did you order your people to attack Temptation and kidnap Cait?"

The tension in her expression increases.

"Did you order them to kill me when they failed to capture her?"

"I would assume from the fact I and my servants here are still alive that you do not believe I—"

The roses in the vase beside her instantly wither and fall in a crumble of black dust to the tabletop. "Answer the question."

Lucretia makes a swift, reassuring gesture toward the tapestries nearby. She doesn't take her eyes from him. "One of the guards I had watching Cait was killed by whomever struck the nightclub," she says, her voice meticulously calm. "The remainder did not see the attackers, but they reported the assault to me moments after it occurred. They have been chastened appropriately for their failure to stop it."

"And the team you sent with me?"

She's silent. He watches her eyes, waiting for the least slip toward the tapestries and the bodyguards he knows she has hiding there. But she's motionless. He can't read the calculations running behind her gaze.

"Lucretia?" he prompts, warning thick in his tone.

Her mouth tightens. "Leave us."

Nothing happens.

"I said leave!"

The tapestries around the room stir. He hears the faint sounds of doors closing. The fabric grows still.

"I promise you," she says carefully. "I did not break our deal."

"Following the assault on Temptation, your people received a call from 'Operations' warning them the attack had failed, after which they attempted to kill me." His brow rises in tacit question.

She looks away. "The situation—"

"The truth, Lucretia."

She glances back at him. "Is complicated."

He's silent.

She seems to take a moment to choose her words carefully. "Recently, I began to receive indications that certain people in my House are, shall we say, not acting in the best interests of Volgert? And, sadly, my attempts to correct this unfortunate lapse in judgment have been less successful than I would have preferred."

"A coup," he translates flatly.

"That is not the word I would prefer to use."

He isn't surprised. The vampire queen of Volgert had taken power with a coup of her own, and she's been ruthless with anyone who would try to replicate the process ever since. Admitting to a conspiracy whose existence she had not immediately been able to crush would be tantamount to admitting that she's lost control of the House she's ruled for over three hundred years.

But the truth is still there, between the lines.

"Who's behind it?" he asks.

She doesn't answer. His brow rises again.

"I am not certain," she concedes like the words are being pulled from her.

"Linden?"

"I do not believe so."

He weighs whether he trusts the response, coming down on the side of "only so far as he has to." "What do you intend to do about it?"

She watches him, and he can predict what she's evaluating. The question of whether he'll help her stop this.

"I don't work for you," he reminds her. "And I won't change that."

"These *nuisances* could kill you next time. You need—"

The sound of a door opening cuts her off. "Mistress?" comes a man's voice from behind the tapestry.

Amar tenses. There's an edge to the man's tone, like alarm under tight control.

Lucretia seems to hear it as well. "Enter," she allows, her voice cautious.

The man pushes past the tapestry. He appears young, maybe twenty, with dark eyes and equally dark skin. Guns are tucked into the holsters strapped to either side of his chest.

"Trouble, Mistress." The young man casts a nervous glance over his shoulder. "Please, I must ask you to evacuate—"

An explosion rocks the building. The chandelier swings wildly, sending its candles toppling to the floor. Lucretia staggers, her hand catching her on the round table.

Amar looks at the door behind him. Shouts carry from beyond the dense wood.

He doesn't waste any more time. "Shadow-cross," he says to the young man. "Now."

The guy shakes his head. "The defenses were the first thing hit. They're flaring out of control. If we try to pass them, they could kill the Mistr—"

Wood shatters behind him. The young man turns, his hands going for his weapons.

Bullets shred through the tapestry. Amar drops to the ground fast while the young man crumples.

In a heartbeat, Lucretia surges across the room, tearing past the tapestry. The fabric falls and a man goes with it, his screams cut short by her ripping hands.

She snarls furiously and whirls away from the fallen body, blood drenching her fingers. He sees bullet wounds in the velvet covering her chest.

Lucretia starts away from the corpse, and then a furious, pained noise escapes her. She staggers.

His confusion lasts only a heartbeat.

"Witch-cursed bullets," she spits. "Those *bastards*. They —" She cuts off with another agonized grunt.

He heads toward the exit. Beyond the fallen tapestry, a doorway opens to a narrow passage inside the wall. A dozen feet ahead, it turns to the right, leaving him blind to any approaching threats.

"If you had anything to do with this, Amar," Lucretia warns from behind him. "I promise you will pay for it. That girl will as well."

"I don't."

She doesn't respond. He glances back to find her watching him, weighing the response.

"I swear," he emphasizes. "Now stay behind me."

Without another word, he strides through the doorway. Past the walls, he can hear the pounding footsteps of people rushing along the corridors. Gunfire follows. Something crashes against the wall, sending a shower of dust raining down from the beams and boards around him. The footsteps race away.

He lets out a breath and keeps moving.

A woman runs around the corner, mist glowing from her hands. But the moment she spots him, she stops, the mist vanishing and her hands raising in a defensive gesture. "Whoa, hey, hold on."

His eyes narrow. "One of yours?" he asks Lucretia without looking away from the woman.

"This doesn't concern you," the succubus says hurriedly. "We're only after Volg—"

Air stirs beside him and silver flashes at the corner of his eye. A knife strikes the woman's midsection, sending her staggering back into the wall.

"No, she isn't." Lucretia pushes past him with her hand still gripping her chest where the bullets tore through. At the woman's side, she drops to a crouch and takes the hilt of the knife. "Who sent you?"

Mist flickers to life around the woman's hands. Lucretia grabs the succubus's wrist, pinning it to the ground, and then she shoves on the blade, cutting further into the woman's insides.

The succubus chokes while the mist flickers and disappears.

He holds his breathing steady, old habits rising to protect him. Any pity for this woman will be taken as a sign of betrayal. Any discomfort will give rise to the idea that he lied when he told Lucretia he had nothing to do with the people attacking the manor. He'd seen worse than this in the years with his father, and he paid dearly until he learned how to bury his reactions.

"Who?" Lucretia repeats.

"Please—"

Lucretia's grip tightens on her wrist, and the succubus shrieks. He hears bones break under the pressure of Lucretia's grasp.

Whimpering with pain, the succubus doesn't answer. Blood soaks her shirt and seeps from the edges of her mouth. She doesn't have much longer to live, even without Lucretia's questions.

And the vampire queen knows it. Sharply, she twists her hold on the woman's broken wrist. *"Who?"*

"Alistair!" the woman screams.

Lucretia releases her grip, a stillness coming over her. But there's a glint to her eyes. A fervor like bloodlust and satisfaction all rolled into one.

It turns his body cold.

"We…" The succubus coughs. Blood spills from her lips. "We'll kill you… vampire bitch."

Lucretia ignores the words, rising to her feet. "I warned you this could happen," she says to him. "You really think you can stay uninvolved?"

He doesn't respond, watching while the last of the succubus's life passes out of her and she sags to the floor. Alistair's succubus. Just another piece on a House chessboard, sacrificed for House purposes.

"That old bastard will tear into the neutrals, same as he's tearing into my people. With that psychic—"

He strides past her, not needing to hear the rest. Disgust rolls through him, tumbling like the magic under his skin and thick with contempt for himself, for Alistair, for Lucretia, and everything that this means. They wanted a war, both of them. For all their protests, for all their claims to the contrary, Alistair and Lucretia were only too eager for it to happen.

And now it's begun.

He fights to keep breathing, even as the possibilities present themselves like images from a nightmare. There hasn't been a war between any of the Houses in nearly fifty years. Skirmishes, yes, but not an all-out war. But his father used to tell stories of it. Tales of the things he'd seen in his childhood. The relish in his voice had been terrible enough, but the images he described, the atrocities he gladly took part in…

And now Linden has a psychic at their disposal.

Chills run through Amar. He'd intended to find this person, to heal them from being Touched and hopefully end the psychic power they have at the same time. He'd intended to secure Cait's safety, and his own as well.

And he'd failed.

His heart pounds in spite of himself. Relative peace between the Houses has been the only thing that allowed him the life he's led since his father died. As long as Linden, Volgert, or any of the Houses hadn't been trying to *annihilate* each other, they'd been willing to accept his assertion that he didn't want the authority and fear his father had commanded. That he only wanted as close to a normal life as he could find. His own power had left the arrangement something of a bargain of mutually assured destruction for any House that would try to force him to join; a simple understanding that he wouldn't kill them if they didn't try to kill him and that, as long as his powers were kept secret, no stupidly ambitious underling could screw that arrangement up.

But all that would be over if they started a war. His *life* would be over, and Cait's would as well. Linden, Volgert— hell, any of them—they'd figure out a way to corral the two of them into a House or kill them because it'd be better than risking someone else gaining use of what he and Cait could do.

All because of this poor, damned psychic.

The thought slows his racing heart. It's still true. Katsuro may have talked of the magic in the world shifting, but that's not what the Houses are fighting about. Not really. The psychic is the key. Without her, Linden and Volgert have nothing to start a war over. And no, that may not stop them entirely now that Alistair sent his people to attack Lucretia in her own home.

But then again, it might.

His feet move faster. There's still a chance. All he has to do is find the psychic. Help her. And keep Linden and everyone else from concluding that he's sided with Volgert in the meantime.

He buries a grimace. That last part might be a problem.

The narrow passage ends, and its exit stands open to a well-appointed library. Swiftly, his eyes sweep over the space, searching for any sign of life. Bookshelves line the walls, and stiff armchairs are placed near a large stained-glass window on the far side of the room. A bulky wooden desk sits near another wall. A glass case displaying large, leather-bound books stands behind it.

But nothing moves. His gaze pauses on the edge of a shadow cast by the moonlight pouring past the stained-glass window. The manor defenses might be down now. If they are, then the simple line of shadow and light is all he needs.

Lucretia makes a tiny grunt behind him, the stifled sound pained. He glances back. Her skin looks too pale, even for a vampire. Tightly controlled agony carves lines on her face.

A rustling from the far end of the room draws his attention instantly.

"Mistress?" The maid peeks over the edge of the desk. She freezes when her wide, red eyes find him. "Oh, M-Master Okoro. My apologies. Please don't hurt—"

Lucretia pushes past him. "Enough, Mira. Where are my bodyguards?"

The relief on the girl's face is immediate. "Mistress! I worried—" She cuts off, seeming to remember the question. "I don't know, ma'am. I-I hid, but I saw some heading for the—"

Her eyes go to the door, and alarm takes the place of her relief. He turns fast, magic rushing through him.

"Hold, please!" a woman cries, her arms raised. Several other people at her back retreat frantically, as if seeking shelter from the wall.

"They're mine, Amar," Lucretia says from behind him.

"And you trust them?" he counters.

She pauses. "Yes."

The ice in his veins dies, obedient as always to his will.

"Jamila," Lucretia continues. "Status?"

For a moment, Jamila continues to eye him as if waiting for the guillotine to drop. "Not good, my lady." Warily, the woman steps farther into the room. Tactical gear covers her, and several guns and knives hang from the belts strapping her hips and chest. The other people with her peer cautiously around the doorframe before coming inside. "Please allow us to escort you to safety. Our people can protect you from here—"

"The defenses," he interrupts.

"Amar," Lucretia says sharply.

He glances over. She meets his gaze, a wealth of threat in her eyes.

"I don't work for you," he tells her quietly.

"But you need me," she counters, her voice equally soft.

He weighs his words for a moment. "I will find this Touched. I will stop them. Our arrangement continues—including the part that protects Cait."

Her eyes narrow.

"The, uh, the defenses have fallen," Jamila offers into the silence. "That's why we must move quickly, my lady, if we're to reach safety before—"

He doesn't wait for more. Swiftly, he strides toward the stained glass window and the edge of shadow and moonlight there.

"No!" Lucretia snaps. "Amar, you—"

The line of shadow falls behind him, and the library is gone.

16

"You seem to have trouble with your hearing, vampire. She's not going."

Sorcha's words carry down the hall. Sitting on a barstool, I don't look away from my study of the water glass in front of me. I know what I'll see if I glance up anyway. Rafael is cleaning the bar while a half dozen mercenaries watch me from various positions around the room. The wolves have been keeping an eye on me all night, and beyond answering my questions about Ulric—he's alive; he's been relocated to a place where the pack can better tend to his injuries—the rest of the group hasn't said a word.

"Our safe houses have remained undetected by the Houses for longer than you've been *alive*." Katsuro this time. He sounds aggravated. "Do you honestly believe that prominent locations such as this can provide her with more protection?"

I trace my finger through the condensation forming on the sides of my glass. Jeans and a long-sleeved shirt cover me now, warmer than the absurd dress and acquired from my apartment by two of the silent, nameless werewolves. My body aches from my run-in with that troll and everything else that happened tonight, bruises gradually making themselves known in what is sure to become a multicolored glory. Meanwhile, it's probably getting close to dawn outside, though you'd never know it in the windowless club. The bomb squad left a few hours back, and most of the cops did too. Only a squad car remains outside, keeping watch on a place they believe is empty and that they locked down—or so Rafael told me when I wandered in here a while ago, having abandoned any hope of sleeping on that narrow camp bed. But the others have been debating the next steps ever since the majority of the cops drove away. The primary problem is that they can't decide where to take me. Katsuro wants us to return to his people, Sorcha refuses to allow him to accompany us any farther, and Bianca just wants me gone from anywhere near her family.

I feel vaguely like a piece of luggage. Or maybe a child, being shuffled between foster homes. Neither is pleasant. I'd leave, except I know I stand a better chance of staying alive with their help, and like them, I don't have any idea of where to go.

This is getting old, though.

"God, would you two just drop it and get her out of here?"

Bianca. I grimace. I haven't heard from Brett, although he's in the other room too. But I've got to figure his opinion is probably similar to his sister's. I can only imagine the public-relations damage control he's going to have to do now that a supposed *bomb* went off at his club.

He probably regrets ever letting me in the door.

"The point is *security*," Sorcha states. "You do not—"

She cuts off, and nothing follows. My brow furrowing, I glance toward the hall.

"Took you long enough," Bianca snaps.

A low voice responds. I can't make out the words, but the sound makes my heart jump.

I shove away from the bar. The mercenaries move immediately to precede me down the dark corridor.

Amar is there.

My feet stop me at the end of the hallway, and I'm staring. I know I'm staring. I have to quit.

But he's *alive*. Alive and here and he's been gone for *days*. He didn't even—

"What?"

Bianca's harsh tone is like a splash of ice water in my face. I flounder under her glare, at a loss for what to say.

Amar isn't helping. He's utterly expressionless and cold, like being here is simply some task he has to attend to before he can move on to other things. He scarcely even pauses to register the fact I'm there before he turns to Bianca and Brett. "Linden has declared war on Volgert. Alistair's forces just attacked Lucretia's manor."

My stomach drops. What?

"How do you know this?" Katsuro says, his tone pointed and slightly poisonous.

Amar gives him a flat look before returning his attention to Brett and Bianca. "You need to make preparations."

Bianca stares at him for a heartbeat and then snags her phone from her pocket. Turning, she strides away while swiping through the screens and then lifting the cell to her ear. "Get my father *now*."

Brett heads past me toward the bar. "Rafael!"

"Cait," Amar calls.

My focus snaps back to him.

"May I speak with you for a moment?"

He sounds like the question is barely an afterthought. I blink, not sure how to take the tone. "Yeah, sure." I cast a quick look around, but there's nowhere to talk. Nowhere the others won't overhear. Anxiously, I start toward the narrow hall leading to the storage room. Amar moves to follow me.

Like a weird entourage, the mercenaries trail us.

"Keep watch," Amar orders them when we reach the hallway.

Sorcha nods. The werewolves stop.

I continue to the storage room and hold the door while Amar walks by me. He doesn't even glance my way. Swallowing hard, I shut the door and then turn back toward him. "What did you need to talk—"

He's right there, and before I can even gasp, he's kissing me. His hands take my face, slide into my hair, and hold me to him like he's afraid I'll vanish. A heartbeat later, he breaks from me. "Are you okay?" he asks roughly.

Blinking, I try to regroup. "Y-yeah, I…" I have no idea what to say. My thoughts are a jumble. My body aches, but I don't care. I want to know why he's been gone so long. I want him to kiss me again.

I opt for the latter. I reach up quickly, pulling him to me, and he doesn't hesitate. In an instant, his lips are on mine. His grip tightens on me, and his body presses me back until I run into the door. I scarcely notice. It only brings him closer, crushing my breasts against his chest. I inhale his scent, all spice and heat and a hint of sweat. It's wonderful. My hands hurry beneath his jacket, relishing his warmth and the sheer fact that he's *here*. With me. Alive. I can feel his heart beating hard in his chest while the kiss deepens. It's like he's trying to drink me in, like he's reminding every cell in his body how this feels.

And I'm right there with him. I'd known I missed him. I don't think I realized how much. It's like the stress, the near-death madness, and everything I've been through in the past hours and days fades to the background—present, yes, but hushed and less painfully vivid now. Because we're together. I'm losing the room and the club and the whole damn town to the simple joy of him against me, near me, here safe with me.

My body presses to his, my legs parting to let one of his own between them. A hungry noise leaves him, tinged with desperation. He pushes harder into me, driving me against his leg and a thrill shoots through my veins. I grind my hips against him. My hands climb beneath his jacket, moving across his powerful muscles and up to his shoulders to keep him close.

He flinches suddenly, making a small hiss of pain. I release him instantly, confused, and his wince doesn't clarify anything. And then my gaze catches on his arm. There's a rip torn through his jacket, right around his upper bicep. The dark fabric makes it hard to be sure, but there's also something dried on the edges of the tear.

It seems like it might be blood.

Alarmed, I look up at him.

"It's nothing," he assures me like he can see the question in my eyes.

I'm not certain I trust the words.

"Are you *sure* you're all right?" he continues. "I heard…" He seems to struggle for a way to explain, and then he pauses, his focus going to his hands in my hair like he's felt something.

I grimace, pulling away a bit. I'd tried to brush out the dried blood. Obviously, I didn't get it all.

"What—" he starts.

"It's fine. It was just—"

"What happened?"

"Kyle. He, um…" I don't know what to say.

"He um what?"

My grimace deepens at the hard edge in his voice. "He shot a guy in front of me."

Amar goes still.

I press onward. "Katsuro's people got me away from him."

"Katsuro."

I nod. "That's why he's here. He followed me. His people stopped Kyle."

Amar looks away, something in his expression like my statement has brought up another problem. "You trust him?"

I hesitate.

"Katsuro," Amar elaborates. "Do you trust him?"

I wish people would stop asking me questions like that, like I'm the Magic Eight Ball of whether someone will stab us in the back. "Why?" I ask.

He takes a second before answering. "I need his help with something."

Okay, that's unexpected. And vague. "Something like what?"

His jaw tightens as if he'd rather not respond.

Anxiety shivers through me. "Amar, something like—"

A knock comes behind me, cutting me off. I retreat to avoid getting bumped by the door when it opens.

Sorcha peeks her head past the opening and then

pauses when she spots us. "My apologies for interrupting."

"What do you need?" Amar replies evenly.

"The others are asking for you," she tells him. "They're—"

"He's down here?"

I tense immediately at the sound of Bianca's voice. Quickly, Sorcha steps aside while Bianca appears at the doorway.

Her gaze twitches between us, icy and yet angry, but her silence lasts only a moment. "There've been more attacks."

My blood goes cold.

"Where?" Amar asks.

Bianca twitches her head to the hall and then moves that way. With a short glance at me, Amar starts after her. I follow him.

Brett and Rafael are waiting beyond the corridor while Katsuro stands near the stairs. They all look so somber, it makes my stomach turn to lead.

"Dad got word right before I called," Bianca says. "Three Volgert strongholds were hit in two different cities. He hadn't heard about Lucretia's manor, but the rest…"

"Linden?" Amar asks.

Bianca nods. "Looks like." Her mouth tightens. "They bombed the *hell* out of them, Amar. Some of them were in populated areas. The locals think it was some kind of terrorist thing but…" Her brow shrugs illustratively. "It's only a matter of time till Volgert retaliates."

Amar turns away, an expression flashing over his face like he's restraining an urge to swear.

"The Touched," Katsuro says. "Does this have anything to do with them?"

Amar glances at him.

Katsuro's brow rises. "Or are you intending to claim you don't know?"

Amar eyes him for a moment longer before returning his focus to the others. "You need to put any relocation plans you have into action. All of you. Whatever you can do to get away from the Houses, it needs to happen now."

"What is it you know, man?" Brett's casual, devil-may-care attitude is completely gone. "What do they have?"

Amar pauses. "A psychic."

I freeze.

Bianca makes an incredulous noise. "A *what*?"

"Some of the Touched are apparently manifesting talents like incubi and succubi. Not all of them, just a few. But this one's done more than that. She can see the future."

"She?" Katsuro interjects.

Amar ignores him. "Her powers are intermittent, according to Lucretia, and what I heard from Alistair confirms that. She doesn't see everything, but he's still using what she *does* see to further his own goals, which includes opportunities to attack his enemies, and which *could* include opportunities to attack us." He pauses. "You all need to get out of here. Take Cait—" Alarm rockets through me at his words. "—and get out of here. Whether or not that psychic sees you is only half the problem. Linden and Volgert *want* a war. Even with the psychic gone, they may not stop, and until we know for certain, it's in your best interests to be elsewhere."

"And what are you going to do?" Bianca snaps.

"Find her. Turn her back if I can."

I stare at him. "She'll see you coming. *Linden* will see you coming."

Amar pauses. "Hopefully not."

A breath leaves me. *Hopefully* not? Is he insane? If there's even a chance—

"What do you know of where Linden keeps their Touched?" Amar asks Katsuro.

My eyebrows climb, his earlier question suddenly clicking. But it's horrible. I don't know whether he can trust Katsuro. Hell, everything I've seen of the guy says he and his people *hate* Amar.

And now Amar wants to work with them?

"Why should we help you?" Katsuro replies, his face inscrutable. "You went to see Lucretia; you came back. If it's true you don't work for her, then that should not have been possible."

"It is if I have a deal with her."

"What *kind* of deal?"

"The kind that allows me to do precisely what I just did. The kind that means I *don't* work for her, and intend to *never* work for her, and am deeply interested in stopping a war in order for that arrangement to continue."

Katsuro's unreadable expression remains. His gaze slides from Amar to me and then back.

Shivers crawl over my skin.

"Linden is hiding the psychic among the regular Touched," Amar presses. "I don't know where, and Lucretia's intel on that didn't pan out. But I want to stop this war, and you want to save this person, which means you and I can help each other. So what information can you offer so we both achieve our interests?"

For a long moment, Katsuro doesn't respond. "We know enough," he concedes finally.

"Locations of storage facilities? Security?"

Katsuro nods once. My stomach churns at the sight.

"Then I'll help you get to her, and if it can be done, I'll help you change her back."

"And after that?" Katsuro replies.

Amar pauses. "We see what she becomes—human or psychic."

Katsuro's displeasure with the response is clear.

"You need me," Amar says. "Without my help, this Touched stays exactly as crazy and helpless as she is right now."

"I need *one* of your kind—and *you're* not the one with the potential ability to pick this psychic from a crowd." Katsuro nods toward me. "Cait comes or there's no deal."

"No," Amar replies immediately.

"This isn't negotiable. She—"

"I said no."

Katsuro regards him. Seconds tick past like screws tightening.

"I'll do it," I blurt into the silence. "I'll go."

The others look at me, alarmed. I don't take my eyes from Amar. I can feel how hard I'm shaking, I can see his anger under that surface of rock, and I know I'm so far into the deep, I couldn't hope to find the shore.

But I don't care. Right now, in this moment, I purely don't care, because if I have even a shred of this weird-ass, people-reading power inside me, I know without a doubt I'm going to use it.

Because I refuse to sit by and risk losing Amar.

"All right, then," Katsuro says. "It's agreed."

For a heartbeat, Amar doesn't move. I can't tell what I'm seeing in the way he's looking at me—rage, ice, something almost pained that I don't understand—but the combination burns. It's everything I can do to hold his gaze.

Sharply, he looks away, his focus snapping to Sorcha. "You're coming too."

It isn't a question. She nods anyway.

"Fine." Amar glances at Bianca. The girl is staring between us like she can't believe our stupidity. He ignores the expression. "Be out of town soon."

Bianca scoffs, but there's not much strength behind the noise. Her jaw works around. "Yeah."

Shaking her head, she turns and walks toward the front of the club.

"Be careful, man," Brett offers dryly. He follows Rafael from the room.

Amar turns back to Katsuro, his gaze skipping past mine. His brow rises coldly.

"We need to meet with my people first," Katsuro says to the unspoken question. "If you want the latest information, anyway."

"Call them. Get the information so we can head out now."

Katsuro chuckles. "And go up against Linden with only you at my back? Not likely."

Amar's expression turns sub-zero.

"You need more forces," Katsuro says. "I need people I can trust. And the clock is ticking." He smiles. "So when do we leave?"

17

WE STEP FROM THE SHADOWS, AND FOR A MOMENT, I THINK we've ended up in a park.

Then my eyes adjust better to the pre-dawn darkness.

I balk. "What the—"

"Over here." Katsuro strides away from us, away from the trees and the streetlight.

And straight into a graveyard. Marble headstones and obelisks dot the grassy expanse ahead of us, their shapes dully illuminated by the ambient light of the city. The glow isn't much, however. I think we're on the edge of old downtown, far from the more commercial areas and the lights there. Trees and bushes ring the property as well, cutting off any view of Corvinson, shadowing the graves, and deadening the sounds of early morning traffic.

I look at Amar, my brow rising with equal parts alarm and incredulity.

A hint of a grimace crosses his face. "It'll be all right," he murmurs, something in his voice like he's hoping the words are true.

He glances at Sorcha and twitches his head for her to go first.

She doesn't bother to hide her displeasure, though it comes with a tinge of nauseated strain. The werewolves shadow-crossed with us this time, escorted by Katsuro and Amar since apparently they don't have that ability themselves. But it's obvious it's one of their least favorite ways to travel.

They all look like they've just gotten off the worst carnival ride in history.

My eyes dart over the graves as Amar and I follow the mercenaries, and my gaze catches on fragments of names and dates while every horror movie I've ever seen plays through my head in utterly unhelpful fashion. I can't believe this, though. Of all the places I thought Katsuro would take us, I definitely hadn't expected this.

I'm walking through a graveyard with a vampire, an incubus, and a pack of werewolves on the way to find a secret society of demons.

An irrational urge to scoff hits me, but there's no humor in the feeling. More like desperation, because madness doesn't even come close to describing my life anymore.

Amar glances at me, questioning. I give him a tight smile.

Leaves rustle up ahead, and my attention snaps toward the sound. Ram steps from behind a mausoleum with several figures following him. At the sight of two of the people with him, I freeze.

"You," Amar says coldly.

"Nice to see you again too, man," Leaf replies.

Blue regards Amar, not saying a word.

"These two work for you?" Amar demands of Katsuro.

"With me," Katsuro confirms. "Yes. How do you think we first learned of you? Of her?" He nods toward me. "We have built a substantial network over the centuries. Our connections are everywhere. And when word reached us that an incubus was looking for information about a Touched, we were curious. As I've said, your kind aren't prone to compassion for others—including, and perhaps most *especially*, those who fall victim to your powers. We wanted to know more, in case it could be useful to us."

I eye Blue and Leaf warily, remembering our visit to their houseboat the other day, when Amar and I had been searching for information on where Volgert was keeping Ruby. Ram had been outside on the docks. That was the first time I'd seen him.

Blue catches me watching her. "I heard you were able to get your friend out of there. She doing okay?"

In my stomach, a pit forms, and I haven't got a clue what to say. No? No, Ruby's not, and I should have seen it because that's what best friends are supposed to do?

That I failed her?

And how she *has* to be okay now because she's gone beyond where I can protect her. Or she has to be *safe*, if nothing else, because I have no idea what I'll do if she's not.

I don't know how to say that here, to this girl I barely know.

Nodding quickly, I manage some fractured attempt at a smile to hide my real reaction. "Yeah."

A pause follows, and I get the impression my efforts were wasted because I'd swear pity flashes in Blue's eyes. But she doesn't say anything beyond: "Good."

"Have you gathered the information I requested?" Katsuro asks.

"Yeah," Leaf replies. "We narrowed down what seems to be the most likely location, but…" He looks reluctant.

"What?" Katsuro prompts.

"It's here," Blue explains. "Corvinson."

"You can't be serious," Amar states.

Blue treats him to a flat look. "Our sources have had their eye on a half dozen different locations around the country, but the old factory out by the train tracks on the east side of Corvinson has every sign of being where they've got this person."

"The factory," Amar says. "You've seen them hiding Touched there?"

"No, but—"

"Lucretia's intel said Linden is keeping this person among the Touched. If none of them are there—"

"That's the *point*," Blue finishes.

My brow knits.

"Linden probably *was* hiding the psychic with the rest of their victims," Blue continues, her voice barbed. "And for all we know, they still have a few there as cover, just in case. We haven't been able to see inside, only to confirm that no Touched have come out. But meanwhile, putting this psychic anywhere near a *known* storage facility isn't exactly the best strategy, is it? That intel is old, so that ship's sailed. Keeping her with the rest now is more like offering her up to be taken, and painting a big-ass target on every location they've got, besides."

"So what have you found?" Katsuro asks.

"Heavy defenses around the factory and a serious lack of any visible reason why. They've also gone out of their way to hide any trace of their presence. You'd never know it's owned by a House. Hell, you wouldn't know it's owned by anyone at all. The defenses appear purely magical, and any Linden forces are staying completely out of sight—if they're even there at all. Our people only learned about it because of a tip from an informant in Linden's ranks."

"Or the information was planted," Amar counters.

"Goddess's sake, man," Leaf protests. "Give us a little credit here. We checked it out."

"If you're scared, incubus," Ram growls. "You're welcome to stay behind."

"I assume you have more evidence," Katsuro cuts in with a placating tone.

"Yeah," Blue agrees shortly. "Alistair is still in town. We've got that. Considering the fact he's taken the risk of installing this super-secret location right on the edge of a neutral city… We think he's keeping this psychic close."

Amar's mouth tightens.

"Sounds like the best option," I offer uncomfortably.

"Agreed," Katsuro says. He glances around at the others. "Are you all ready to leave?"

Blue hesitates. "Dawn's in an hour. If we wait till tonight—"

"The psychic might be gone," Katsuro interjects. "We have this opportunity; we need to take it. The longer we wait, the more chance they'll move her elsewhere."

Blue glances at Leaf uncomfortably and then nods. "Yeah, all right."

The others around us signal their agreement too, though a couple of them look as discomfited as Blue. Suddenly, I find myself wondering what happens to vampires—*real* vampires—when they come in contact with sunlight.

I can guess from their expressions that it isn't good.

"If the other Touched aren't there," Amar says, "you don't need Cait to come."

"True," Katsuro allows. "But they *might* be, in which case nothing has changed."

Amar is silent for a moment. "Your people go in first."

Katsuro smiles. It doesn't reach his eyes. "Of course. For Cait's sake. Though if we should run into trouble, I do hope we can count on your assistance—*whatever* form that might take."

Amar doesn't respond. A second creeps by, and then another.

Katsuro's expression takes on a deadly edge. "Move out," he orders his people. He glances at me, the poisonous look vanishing. "If you'll follow us?"

I glance between them, but there's nothing for it. Katsuro is watching me, waiting, and I get the impression Amar wouldn't answer any questions I could ask anyway.

Swallowing hard, I nod and follow the others, Amar staying close to my side.

⌑

OUR CARAVAN OF SUVS PULLS OVER ON A DARKENED STREET on the far end of town. We hadn't shadow-crossed. The trolls can't, so Katsuro tells me. I don't think doing so would have helped me feel any less nervous, but at least it would have gotten the trip over faster.

Trying to keep myself from trembling with steadily building anxiety, I climb from the back of the black vehicle. Katsuro's group brought six of the things. It's eerie, all these apparent resources. These people on his side. I know he saved my life and seems to be only interested in helping people.

But I'm still wondering who the hell he might actually be. It's not like he ever answered that question. He only ever says that it's complicated.

I wish I knew what that might mean.

The rest of his people climb from the SUVs in silence and, in between scanning the area around us, I can see the vampires anxiously eyeing the sky. In the moonless depths, a few clouds have started to become visible, hinting that morning is on its way.

"Two blocks in that direction and a hundred yards to the right," Blue whispers to Katsuro, pointing farther down the narrow alley.

Katsuro nods. "I want one team up top to keep watch and another to take the side. Find a rear entrance and another way for us to leave in case shadow-crossing isn't an option."

The others nod their assent.

Katsuro turns toward me. "Stay close. It is imperative that Linden not get their hands on you. Therefore, if anything happens, I want you to do everything you can to leave immediately, no matter what you see. Agreed?"

Shivers quiver through my midsection. He's looking at me like Amar and the others aren't even here. Like I'm his responsibility to protect.

I don't know what else to do but nod.

His gaze flicks to Sorcha and the werewolves, and then lands a heartbeat longer on Amar.

"Ready?" he says to Ram like nothing happened.

The big guy nods. Katsuro echoes the motion and then heads for the door.

I can see Amar's glower when he comes up beside me. Without a word, he walks after the others. I trail him, eyeing the buildings around us worriedly. The few streetlights create pools of light and shadow that look infinitely threatening. I can't hear most of the people around me walking. Vampires and werewolves alike, they're deathly silent.

It feels lonely and creepy all at the same time.

We round a corner.

"Hold," Ram whispers.

Most of Katsuro's people stop, and we do too. Tank and several other enormous people who have to be trolls continue to Ram's side.

Ram glances over the rest of us as if checking to make certain everyone has obeyed his command, and then he and the other trolls start forward again in silence. But nothing else happens. My brow furrows in confusion. Why did he want us to—

The air around the trolls shimmers like the iridescent surface of a soap bubble.

My eyes go wide. Ram and his companions keep going. Striding forward, they continue through air that has started roiling like water on the boil—at least beyond them. Right where they are, the chaos seems to clear, like they're holding back the impossibly shimmering air with the sheer force of their presence. But each step farther seems to be coming with difficulty. I can see them breathing hard while, one by one, they come to a halt like they're forming a line.

Ram stops last. Effort lining his face, he casts a quick look back to us.

"Go," he growls.

Katsuro and his people dart forward. Ducking low, they skirt past the trolls' sides like they're hurrying through a tiny tunnel.

Which is basically what seems to be happening.

"Come on," Amar says.

He doesn't wait for my response. Taking my hand, he pulls me onward. Static brushes my skin, growing stronger and making the hairs on my arms stand on end. The air hisses and snaps like an electrical circuit on the verge of breaking. My heart pounding, I duck while Amar does the same.

And we rush forward.

My skin crawls with electricity, and the air feels burned. My feet crunch fast over the gravel, and unbidden, the thought of what might happen if I trip flashes through my mind. What lies beyond this tiny tunnel of safety held up by trolls?

Before I can find out, we're past Ram and the air clears. Still hanging onto my hand, Amar runs to the cover of a nearby building, where Katsuro and his people are already waiting. Sorcha and her companions come after us, their attention locked on our surroundings.

But nothing moves. When Ram and the other trolls leave the strange wall of electricity, even the air returns to its ordinary state of calm.

Katsuro glances at Blue, his brow twitching up. She gives a small shake of her head.

His mouth tightens, and then he motions to his people. Without a word, they split up. Two groups head away from us. Katsuro nods to several of the remaining people. In silence, they slip from the cover of the shadows and dart toward a building up ahead.

They reach the door. A heartbeat passes in which they seem to be picking the lock, and then the weighty metal thing swings open.

No alarms go off. No shouts ring out.

Sorcha tenses beside me. I look at her.

She's wincing. So are the other mercenaries beside her. At my glance, she touches her nose, a disgusted look on her face.

My confusion clears. She smells something.

Katsuro motions for the others to go on ahead, but from the way his eyes flick to Sorcha, I can tell he's caught her gesture too.

We head for the door.

A smell like rotten meat greets us from a dozen yards away.

My stomach tries to flee by way of my throat. I choke it back down, fighting to draw in air. Oh God.

The vampires eye us warily. They don't breathe, I realize. They can't smell this at all.

Lucky.

Taking the shortest breaths possible, I continue after the others. My eyes are stinging by the time I reach the door. The darkness when I follow the others inside is impressive, but right away, it's obvious somebody is still paying for electricity around here. An exit sign flickers in the distance, though two of its four letters are mostly blacked out. E. I. It feels like some esoteric code, signifying who knows what.

The dim red glow thins the shadows, though, revealing what looks like a room—a large one. I can't find the ceiling in the darkness, and there aren't any walls on either side of us. Hulking shapes occupy the expanse between us and the exit sign. Machinery, maybe. Most of it seems broken; I can't be sure.

But that's not all. My gorge rises when I spot the carcasses heaped on the floor. Cows, I think. Or horses. In the shadows, it's hard to tell.

Suddenly, the vampires flinch, their footsteps coming to

a stop. At my side, Sorcha halts too, a pained look on her face.

I'm lost. What is it now?

The other werewolves turn fast, their gazes darting around like they're scanning the walls with the intent of killing them. Someone takes my arm. I barely stop myself from jumping a mile.

Katsuro is there.

"What?" I mouth desperately.

He glances on toward Amar, who reaches up and taps his ear with a questioning look. Katsuro nods.

Sound. I can't hear anything, though.

Right.

My confusion turns to dread. Something beyond the normal human range of hearing, then, and obviously, I don't have that. But the vampires and werewolves do. Between that and the dead animals still trying to make me lose my lunch, the implication is clear.

Somebody prepared for this. Us. The place is crawling with measures to hide something from werewolves, vampires, and goodness knows who else. But beyond the sound and smell, no one is attacking. Everybody around me is studying our surroundings like they can see far better than me, and given everything else that's happened so far, I have no reason to doubt they can. They don't seem to spot any threats, however. It's only this. Magical barriers. Rotting carcasses. Some horrible noise I can't hear.

And a clattering.

I start to turn. I hear somebody shout.

A blinding light bursts across the world, and a deafening noise comes with it. In an instant, the darkness turns to day, only to plunge back to black, and I can't see. Can't hear. I don't know what's going on.

Someone slams into me, bearing me down to the ground. I tumble, my hands flying out on instinct, and fire scorches across my palms when they hit the floor. Sounds start to penetrate the ringing in my ears. Popping noises. So many popping noises. And screams.

I gasp, blinking in a desperate attempt to clear the stars from my eyes. Sorcha is there, holding me down. We're behind something bulky. Some of the machinery, I think.

A figure rushes past only to stumble like they've been hit by something, and then they're gone, staggering out of view. I can't tell who it was. What happened.

I can guess.

Sorcha's grip disappears, and then Amar is at my side. His mouth moves. The words are lost to the whine in my ears, but I can read his lips. *Come on.*

Not waiting for an answer, he hauls me up from the ground. I look for Sorcha, but she's not there. Not as a human, anyway. Where she had been, a huge wolf now stands.

She looks back at me, her hackles raised, her massive form silhouetted in the faint light. Her amber eyes glow, fierce and terrifying like they're lit by a fire inside. She makes a barking motion, almost like a shout for us to go.

Amar takes off. I stagger away from Sorcha, struggling to stay by his side. With his arm around me like a shield, he pulls me with him while he races through the narrow paths formed between the machinery. I can't tell where we're going. I can barely even see.

And then a wall arrives. A door. Amar grabs the handle, and whatever is locking it shatters. It's like déjà vu of the other night.

He yanks the door wide, but unlike the other night, no empty hallway greets us this time. Instead, there are emergency lights and people with guns aimed right at our chests. In the yellow glow, I see their eyes go wide behind their ski masks. Their hands clench on their weapons.

A wave of ice rushes around me, burning with static, invisible as the air. Every nerve of my body flies instantly to high alert, as if some sixth sense from primordial times has suddenly started shrieking that I'm in mortal danger.

The people ahead of us crumple like marionettes with slashed strings.

Amar doesn't hesitate. Still holding onto me tightly, he hurries around them and brings me along.

I stagger after him, but I can't take my gaze from the people on the ground. They haven't moved. They're probably unconscious.

But every instinct I possess is screaming that something so much more horrible has happened.

We reach a corner, and Amar pushes me back against the shelter of the wall. Quickly, he peers past the turn. "We'll shadow-cross to the outside," he tells me. "I'll figure out a way to get us past the barriers once we're there."

"What…" I gasp.

He glances at me. My eyes twitch from him to the fallen people and back again.

His mouth tightens. "Outside." Pulling me with him, he races into the next stretch of hall.

Three people rush around a corner ahead, guns raised. I hear the gunshot. Feel something sting the side of my face.

And the wave of cold returns—stronger, faster, ripping around me like I've become a rock in a torrential river of razor-edged ice, and in it, I freeze. I can't breathe from the force. From the power serrating the world around me.

The attackers topple. From the corner of my eye, I see

Amar cast a quick glance at me, and then we're moving again. I can't hear gunfire anymore. I can't hear anything but the sound of my own gasping breaths.

I stumble to a stop when we come closer to the fallen people. My arm yanks from Amar's grasp of its own accord.

They're dead. They *have* to be dead. Their eyes stare emptily at the ceiling, their mouths are slack with horror, and their guns… sweet God, what happened to their *guns*? The metal has crumpled in on itself like tinfoil.

No chance anyone could use them to shoot at us now…

"Cait." Amar takes my arm again, trying to keep me moving. "Come on."

I tear my eyes from the bodies and the weapons, only to stare at him. And I have no words. He… he killed them. With a thought. With a look.

Has he told you what he is?

Rumors of what he can do…

Monster…

I push away and stumble back from Amar, my hands raised like they stand a chance in hell of protecting me.

Desperation tinges his expression. His eyes flash to the hall. "Please. They'll be coming. We have to—"

I stifle a shriek, but the sound cuts him off. Shaking hard, I draw a ragged breath. "What… what—"

I can't get past the word. And I have to get out of here. Away from this building, these demons…

Him.

I stop at the thought, my blood running cold for a whole new reason. Do I want that?

Do I *really* want that?

My insides shake like I've been frozen to my core. Do I want to run with no chance for an explanation? To give into my fears and decide that, yes, Amar is the monster everyone else has claimed him to be?

Or do I trust what I've seen? What I've felt? Do I trust… me?

I draw a tiny breath. This is madness. I'm being an idiot. I'm trusting my gut, my fallen-for-a-guy-I-*clearly*-don't-know-enough-about gut, over the whole damn world.

It's insane.

"*Please*, Cait," Amar begs.

Insane, and possibly my only chance of making it out of this building alive.

"Let's go," I say, my voice choked.

Amar pauses like the words have taken him by surprise. "Okay."

He begins to reach for my hand only to reconsider when I flinch, not quite retreating from him. Another heartbeat passes.

"Right," he allows, and in spite of everything, the pained note in his voice hurts. He nods to the corridor, dropping his eyes from mine. "This way."

❧

WE DON'T MAKE IT TO THE NEXT TURN BEFORE SOMEONE ELSE barrels into the hall.

"Don't!" Ram shouts, his hands flying up.

And nothing else happens.

Paralyzed, a cry trapped behind my bloodless lips, I twitch my eyes to Amar. He hasn't moved. Not a single thing about him hints at what he could have done if it hadn't been Ram ahead of us.

And that's terrifying.

Ram lowers his hands slowly and glances at the people with him as if checking to make sure they're still alive. "Katsuro's found her," he tells us shortly.

Amar starts toward him, and nervously, I follow.

"We're securing the area," Ram states. "Our people found the defense controls and have them in hand. Your wolves are sweeping the rest of the property, and they don't seem too happy about the defenses Linden put in place to slow them down." His metal teeth glint when he gives a cold grin. "I think they're taking it out on whatever stragglers they find."

He makes a curt gesture back the way he came and then begins walking in that direction.

I try not to notice how the others watch Amar as much as the hallway while we follow Ram. I know Ram said there were only rumors about what Amar could do, but from the way they're all looking at him, I wonder how terrifying the stories were.

And how close they were to the truth.

We reach another door, and Ram steps aside, motioning for us to go on ahead. I trail Amar past the doorway, working hard to hide my anxiety.

Then I see the inside of the room, and I fail miserably.

There aren't any other Touched. No one at all, save for Katsuro and his people.

And a girl.

She's in her late teens or maybe younger, but she sits on the floor with her legs curled under her like a child. With a finger, she's tracing abstract designs in the dust. Scrubs like a nurse would wear cover her. The khaki fabric is smudged with dirt, and the seam by her left shoulder is ripped. Her long red hair hangs around her face in a tangled mess; a strand of it is caught on her mouth, but she gives no sign of noticing. She's humming a tuneless song while mist floats from her like steam, all weird and wrong and making my eyes ache. But it's not the only terrible thing.

A thick metal collar encircles her neck as if she's an attack dog more than a human being. From either side of the collar, large chains run to heavy bolts in the wall. The metal rattles every time she moves.

She spots us. A happy, burbling noise leaves her, and her cornflower blue eyes go wide. But it doesn't last. After only a heartbeat, her gaze ambles away, climbing the walls, drifting over the ceiling, lighting back on us briefly and then losing focus again. Her hands skitter over the floor, abandoning the abstract patterns, and they don't seem to be in sync with the rest of her body. They spasm and twitch; they chase each other around on the grit and concrete. She doesn't even seem aware of their motions.

"Kitty?" she calls. "Kitty? Marbles in the partridge tree." Animal noises follow, grunts and squeaks that return to speech a moment later. "Are they squishy? Who's climbing the mountain?"

I shudder. Oh my God, we have to fix this.

"So?" Katsuro prompts.

Amar gives him a flat look and then strides toward the girl. The same happy, burbling sound escapes her again, and the twitching of her hands speeds up. One of them skips toward Amar, making scrabbling motions.

He glances briefly to her chains and the bolts on the wall and then sinks down just beyond the full reach of her arms.

"Shiny? Shiny? Shiny?" She says the word over and over, her body rocking with each repetition. The anticipation on her face makes my skin crawl.

Amar lets out a breath and then extends a hand. His fingers wrap around her wrist.

Her eyes snap to his, cold and piercing. "You'll kill her, you know."

Amar jerks away like he's been burned. The girl's icy expression vanishes. She gnaws on her lip while her gaze loses focus again, her attention wandering off like she's tracking something across the floor.

For a moment, Amar doesn't move. I can't even see him breathing. And then, slowly, he reaches out to grasp her wrist again.

Her excitement lasts less than a heartbeat this time, and her eyes go wide as a surge of static fills the room. The electric sensation fades quickly; it feels almost as if it's being brought back under control. But the girl clearly doesn't like it. Short, angry noises leave her, and her free hand grips her arm, trying to yank it from Amar's grasp.

He doesn't let go. Her motions become more frantic. More terrified. Her noises transform into animal-like screeches, and she lurches as if she's being shocked. Her head thrashes, the tangles of her red hair whipping around her face. Her other hand flails out, clawing at the concrete behind her, trying to drag her away from him.

And it doesn't stop. The struggle, her frightened expression, none of it. Instead, she begins to choke like she's swallowing her own tongue.

With a muttered curse, Amar releases her. "It's not working. I can't…" He shakes his head.

I falter, watching the girl. In ragged gasps, her breathing slows, though small keening noises leave her. She rocks back and forth as if comforting herself, but in only a moment, her hands begin twitching as they had before.

"Okay," I allow. "But... now what?"

Guardedly, Amar glances at Katsuro. "We can't leave her for the Houses."

"And I won't leave her as she is," Katsuro replies.

Amar meets his gaze. A grimace twists his face a moment later.

Chills creep through me when I read between the lines. "You can't *kill* her." My stomach rolls. "Please. Amar, I don't know what you—" I can't finish the sentence. I can't deal with that right now. "She's the *victim* here. We can't—"

The bitter resolve on both their faces isn't shifting. Beyond them, I can see Leaf and Blue, their fangs already peeking over their lips and their expressions much the same.

It makes me want to put myself between them and this girl.

I look back at her. She's mumbling to herself about butterflies, and tracing patterns through the gravel bits on the floor like a child finger-painting.

But I can see it, that mist around her. The horrible wrongness of it, like a poisonous creature with its tentacles woven into her skin.

And more than that.

I start toward her.

"Cait," Amar protests.

I ignore him. I can see... something. Her, I think. The girl past the madness, *before* the madness. It makes my head hurt, as if my eyes are sending messages my brain can't interpret. But it's like the other girl at the hospital. Like Ruby too, a bit—though I'd been so upset I didn't really pick up on it then.

She's still there.

"Dammit, Cait, don't—"

"Let her," I hear Katsuro say from behind me. "Please."

I crouch down just beyond the limits of the girl's leash. She doesn't look up, but an excited grin twitches over her face. She seems to have forgotten about Amar's attempt completely. As if operating on its own, one of her hands lurches toward me. Her other hand moves, snagging it and pulling it back to the task of tracing swirls in the dust.

"Flap-flap." She giggles. "Pretty butterflies, flap-flap."

I struggle to ignore the words and the fact I don't really know what I'm doing, and I reach out cautiously to rest my fingers on her arm. The excited twitching on her face increases. I struggle to ignore that too. I know the Touched want what we can give them. That they can feel the magic inside us. And at any moment, she might attack.

But she's chained and I have to try.

My head throbs while I clasp her wrist. Something is there, beyond the toxic mist. Something weird. Cold, yet with flashes like fire. But it's not the same as this fog around her, and like the hospital girl, if I just reach out… if I just push back on that wretched, stinging mist like *this*…

The girl gasps, her cornflower blue eyes flying wide, and she starts to recoil. As quickly as I can, I grab her arm with my other hand to keep her from retreating. A choked shriek leaves her, but she freezes, her gaze locked on me. Pain twists over her face, and then horror too. It hurts to see. Who knows what this girl went through? What the goddamned House of Linden *put* her through?

But the mist is retreating. Changing. Going back inside her like it did with the girl from the hospital. Shuddering breaths leave her while it vanishes. Like a ragdoll, she sags to the ground.

I release her arm, my heart pounding as if I just ran a

mile in a minute. My head spins, and I reach out, trying to brace myself on the roiling concrete.

Hands grab my shoulders. Pull me up from the ground and away from the girl. I look over, finding Amar.

"Cait?"

"I'm all right." With effort, I straighten and take a step farther from him.

He lets me go. From the corner of my eye, I can see the discomfort on his face.

I turn away.

The girl starts moving, drawing my attention. She's still seated on the ground, but she's looking around like she's trying to figure out where the hell she's ended up. And then her bright blue gaze lands on us.

My brow twitches down. Something still feels wrong. I don't know what it—

"You," the girl gasps. Her eyes dart across Katsuro's people. Amar. "I know you. All of you. In the dream, you…" Alarm crosses her face. She looks away from us.

I glance at Katsuro and Amar, lost.

"It *worked*," the girl breathes.

Confusion hits me. Huh?

"I *saw* you," she continues, a shaky grin taking the place of her alarm. "I knew you'd come. I never told him. I kept it secret. But I *knew*. And—"

Her brow furrows sharply, and she flinches, staring at the ground for a heartbeat like she's seeing something in the concrete. And then, just as abruptly, she looks up again.

Straight at me.

"Hiding won't save you," she says.

My sense of something wrong grows a hundredfold. My skin crawls like it's covered in ants, and suddenly, I want to be as far from this girl as possible. It's like the weirdness I felt beneath the mist. Like the cold and the fire. But not the same. Not exactly.

Amar's hand takes my upper arm, and I jump, realizing I've started to retreat. I tug my gaze from the girl to find him studying me. He's picked up on my unease; I'd swear by it. But he doesn't say anything, looking instead at Katsuro.

"Still there," Amar comments quietly.

Katsuro meets his eyes. I shiver at the tension there, and at the question hanging in the air of what happens next.

But then Katsuro turns to me. "What's wrong?" he asks flatly.

My head shakes. "I'm not sure. I—"

"Who are you?"

I blink, my attention snapping back to the girl. She's staring at us.

"You were in my dream," she continues, her voice like a frightened child. "The horrible, *horrible*—"

Her brow furrows, and her eyes drop away like she's fighting off a terrible memory. The sight sends a pained sensation through me. It's so similar to that expression Ruby had when her mind went back to what Volgert put her through.

"We're here to help you," I manage.

She looks up at me fearfully. "Help?"

"We're going to get you out of here. Back to your family or… you know." I shrug awkwardly. "Someplace safe."

She stares at me for a heartbeat, and it's everything I can do not to run. It's her eyes. Something about her eyes. I can't put my finger on what—

"You're not human." The girl turns toward Katsuro. "You're… Are you monsters?"

"No." Katsuro's voice is placid as a windless lake. "And no. We've come to help you, that's all." He pauses. "What's your name, child?"

She bites her lip briefly. "Penny Campbell."

"It's a pleasure to meet you, Penny. If you would allow us, may we remove those chains?"

My heart rate flies higher. That's a bad plan. I have no idea *why*, but I know—I just *know*—it's a bad plan.

Something's wrong with her eyes. *In* her eyes.

Katsuro's gaze flicks to me, fast and then gone, but I get the impression my nascent panic attack hasn't escaped his notice. Without a word being spoken, his people shift their positions ever so slightly to better surround Penny. At the same moment, Katsuro nods to Ram, who goes toward her.

The girl lifts her chin cautiously, watching Ram like she's afraid he'll bite. In a sharp motion, Ram pulls the collar apart, breaking the lock, and then he returns to Katsuro's side.

Rubbing her neck, Penny looks at Katsuro. "So… can I get out of here?" A thread of desperation runs through her voice. "Please?"

"Of course," Katsuro replies evenly. "We just need to make certain it's safe first."

Her brow furrows. Her gaze twitches over the others. "O-okay. Um…"

She moves to rise, her pale hands bracing her on the concrete, but her legs buckle like a newborn fawn. With a frightened gasp, she stumbles. One of Katsuro's people reaches out to catch her before she hits the ground.

Everything happens too fast. She tumbles against the

man. He staggers. And then, somehow, she's standing upright and the gun from the guy's belt has ended up in her hand.

Aimed at Amar.

"Don't try it," she warns him. "I won't miss like those ones at the little house in the woods did. I know I won't. You do anything with that wicked curse of yours, and you'll be dead before I hit the ground."

She grins as if she'd actually enjoy proving her ability to do exactly what she's said. And in an instant, I realize what I've been seeing.

There's *nothing* in her eyes. Her face says one thing, and on the surface, her eyes do too. And it looks real—*so* real.

But it's not.

Beneath that surface, beneath whatever is on her face at the moment, there's just… nothing. It's like every emotion, every reaction, every expression is simply a theater mask she's picking up and then setting aside as convenience dictates.

While there's only a soulless void underneath.

"What is this?" Katsuro demands. "Why are you—"

"Because I want to," Penny interrupts like it's obvious. "That's what your kind—sorry—" She giggles. It sets my teeth on edge. "*Our* kind. That's what we do, isn't it? *Whatever* we want, to *whomever* we want. That's why I'm here. Some monster—and you're *all* monsters—decided to do this to me for *fun*."

She shudders, her humor vanishing like it never existed. "So now *I'm* going to have fun. The doctors called me a monster too, and I think I'll prove it. It's just a word pathetic people use to describe those they fear, after all." She smiles coldly. "I'm going to tear this big ol' world of monsters into itty-bitty pieces, and I'm going to watch it burn like pretty little butterflies glowing in the sky. I know what's coming, after all. I've seen it changing up this world in a way no one's witnessed in a thousand years." Her expression reminds me of a hyena. "And I can't wait."

Not taking her eyes from Amar, she backs toward the door. Katsuro's people glance at their leader and then silently retreat, giving her space.

She reaches the door and tugs it open without looking at it. "Let me tell you something, Death," she says to Amar. "You're not going to kill me. I'm sure of it. Do you know why?"

Penny glances at me. Her grin returns, bright as a photo flash.

And she pulls the trigger.

Amar staggers. Without a heartbeat's hesitation, she swings the gun toward me, and I hear another gunshot. But instantly, Katsuro slams into me, and then the ground does too. Pain bursts through my arm, my side, and all the air rushes from my chest. The weight on me shifts and vanishes quickly, and I hear more gunfire and people shouting, but I'm just looking for Amar. I have to find Amar.

He's on the ground.

A strangled cry escapes me. I scramble toward him on hands and knees because standing will take too damn long, and then my palms land in blood. His blood.

Oh God, please no.

He gasps. He's gripping his midsection, and agony lines his face. People are moving around me, but I barely see them. Frantic, I press my hands to his, trying to hold the wound closed. Blood wells between my fingers.

"Amar," I beg. "Please, Amar, just—"

Someone crouches beside me and attempts to move me

aside. I shriek, struggling to shoulder them away without taking my hands from him. And they're yelling at me, this person. Yelling muffled words that make no sense.

I look up.

"Cait!" Leaf glares at me. "You have to let me—"

I choke on a scream.

"Please." Blue appears on the other side of me. "We can—"

"Don't you touch him!" I shout. "You're not feeding on—"

Blue grips my arm. I can't shake off her grasp. "We won't," she says firmly. "But Leaf was a doctor before he was turned, and he needs to help Amar right now."

I stare at her. It takes a moment before I can make myself trust the words enough to move.

Leaf takes my place immediately. Blue draws me away with her and helps me rise to my feet. With more strength than it seems like she should have, she pulls me around.

With effort, my eyes focus on the rest of the room.

People are coming back through the door, frustration on their faces. Katsuro is talking to them. Shouting, really. Ram is on his cell phone. The thing looks tiny in his fist, and from the rage on his face, I'm amazed he hasn't crushed the device.

Katsuro turns toward me, and my brows climb. Bullet wounds puncture the side of his chest. I don't see much in the way of blood, but— "You're hurt," I sputter.

He glances at the wounds briefly. "Better me than you."

"Did they find her?" Blue asks.

He hesitates. "They will." His gaze flicks over the rest of the room before returning to Blue. "Get Cait out of here."

"No," I protest immediately. "I have to stay with—"

"We'll take care of Amar. Just go."

I falter at the insistence in Katsuro's eyes, and chills run through me when I think of the reason why. Penny could still be here. Or she could be waiting outside.

Or anything.

I nod. "O-okay. But you have to get him out of here too. Please."

Blue's grip on me tightens. Over my shoulder, I cast a glance at Amar. Leaf is still crouched beside him. I can't be sure, but it looks like he's managed to slow the bleeding.

"He'll be right behind us," Blue promises.

I try to believe the words while she draws me over a line of shadow and the room disappears.

1 8

Hours have passed, or maybe years, while I sit on this hard plastic chair in a veterinary clinic waiting room, my bandaged hands wrapped around a Styrofoam cup of coffee that's long since gone cold. The lights are mostly off but for a single panel glowing over the empty front desk, and the closed blinds dim the sunlight from outside to a muted gray. A television plays the news in the corner. There aren't any reports about what happened at the factory, though. Only stories of some unexplained fire at a dive bar across town.

I shift on the seat, my muscles and bruises aching. The bitter, musky smell of too many animals in a small space stings my nose. Sorcha has taken the chair beside me, while Blue stands by the hallway leading farther back into the clinic. I can't decide if the vampire girl is a guard to keep me from going back there or a liaison for whatever Leaf needs to report.

Amar is in surgery. It's all I know. Blue brought me here, swearing the place was owned by a friend of

Katsuro's and that the Houses wouldn't know we'd arrived. People have been appearing and disappearing through doors and shadows ever since, some of them wearing scrubs, others carrying coolers bearing official-looking markings. I don't know who they are. How they fit into this bizarre network of connections Katsuro claims he has. They're helping Amar, Blue tells me. But that's all I've heard.

The shadows by the corner play tricks on me, and suddenly, Katsuro strides into the room. "Anything?" he asks.

Blue shakes her head.

I shiver. My eyes track Sorcha while she rises to her feet and walks to the front window. Despite her transformation earlier, she still has the same clothes—a mystery I don't have the energy to explore right now. Staying out of sight behind a wall, she pulls a single strip of the mini blinds aside to check our surroundings.

"My people will make certain this place stays secure," Katsuro assures her. "We have the whole area under surveillance."

She gives him a flat look before returning to take the seat by my side. And for some reason, I'm comforted. I know she's just doing her job, staying near me. That Amar paid her and that's the only reason she's here.

But it doesn't change the feeling.

A door somewhere down the hallway opens. I look toward the sound, my heart climbing my throat.

Leaf walks from the corridor, and I can't read his expression. I can't tell what's happened, and it terrifies me.

"So...?" Blue prompts carefully.

Leaf glances at her. I'm paralyzed.

"He's stable."

A shuddering breath leaves me in a rush. "Can I see him?"

Leaf nods. "Yeah."

I set the cup down quickly and hurry toward him. He hesitates when he sees Sorcha follow me, but the pause lasts only a moment.

"This way." He starts down the hall again.

It's hard not to rush ahead, but I don't know what room Amar is in.

I wish Leaf would walk faster.

"He was lucky," Leaf tells me. "The damage could have been much worse. He'll need to rest, and it'll be slow going for a little while, but he's a demon. We bounce back."

Leaf smiles. I nod, trying and pretty much failing to return the expression. Without another word, he opens the door at the end of the hall.

Amar is lying on a metal table, a pale blue blanket over him. Another bundle of blankets are tucked under his head as a pillow.

But he's awake, and seeing his dark eyes looking at me when I walk through the door sends a jolt of relief through me so powerful, it makes me want to cry.

"Hey," he says, his voice rough. He appears exhausted.

Another breath presses from my chest. I cross the room in a heartbeat, only to freeze at the side of the makeshift bed. I want to touch him. Hug him. Kiss him. But I'm scared. Machines surround him, and strange tubes too. I'm terrified I'll bump one of them and make something horrible happen.

"Hey," I manage.

The corner of his mouth rises in a small smile. "I'm all right, Cait. Promise."

I swallow hard and nod, pouring everything I've got

into making my expression look like I believe the words.

Rather than showing vestiges of the worry that's spent the better part of the day eating me alive.

A flicker of consternation passes across Amar's face like he's picked up on my anxiety for him anyway. But he doesn't say anything, his gaze instead going beyond me to the door.

I look back over my shoulder. Leaf is gone, but Katsuro stands in the doorway. Sorcha eyes him from her position in the hall.

"Glad to see you're doing better," the vampire says, ignoring her.

Amar pauses. "Thank you… for all this."

Katsuro nods.

"So now what happens?" I ask. "Penny's out there, and she's…" I don't know how to describe what I saw. "I mean, she's…"

"Insane," Amar summarizes.

"Is it something I did?" I ask, putting words to one of the countless fears that have been gnawing at me for hours. "Pushing back the mist or doing it wrong or… Her eyes are *empty*. There's *nothing* in them. It's like she's—"

"I had my people do some digging," Katsuro cuts in. "Trawl the internet; make some calls." He pauses. "It wasn't you."

I want to be relieved, but I can't. Not after what I saw at that factory. Not when the look on Katsuro's face is making my stomach twist with dread.

"The name she gave us, Penny Campbell? I thought I might have heard it before. It turns out Penelope 'Penny' Campbell was on the news about three years ago—or, rather, her family was. They died in a house fire Penny confessed to setting when she was fifteen. Seems her mother grounded her for cutting off her nine-year-old sister's ponytail in a fit of pique, and in retaliation, Penny waited till they'd all gone to bed and then doused the furniture with gasoline from the garage. Set the fire, locked the doors, and then watched the house burn from across the street while eating a plate of cookies she made specifically for the occasion. Killed the whole family: brothers, sister, parents. She was sent to a psychiatric hospital in Florida, where she stayed until Alistair's people found her. I suppose Linden figured that the *already* insane—and violently so—would be more aggressive as Touched and therefore more valuable in the pit matches to which they are sent."

I stare at him, at a loss for what horrifies me more in what he just said.

And for the fact that I set this person loose.

Katsuro looks briefly to Sorcha and then steps farther into the room, letting the door swing closed behind him. "Cait says I can trust you," he continues to Amar. "And everything I have seen indicates she might very well be right, so that is what I am going to do. I told you both the answer to who we are is complicated, and that is the truth. But it is also dangerous. There are people who would kill us for who and what we are."

I shiver, remembering the salvage yard.

"You met some of them," Katsuro says, as if reading my reaction. "The ones who call themselves the Guardians. They worship a warped memory of the powers that ruled this world before the Houses ever existed. They distort the idea of what those forces stood for, what they were." He pauses. "They distort *us*."

"The original Guardians were destroyed," Amar says. I hear the alarm beneath the carefully controlled tone of his voice. "A thousand years ago, their Council and all their supporters were wiped out. All that exist now are copycats and lunatics."

"Most of the Thirteen were killed, yes," Katsuro acknowledges. "But I was not. I survived the rebellion, the Houses' scourge, and as one of the last remaining members of the original Guardian Council, I have spent the better part of the past millennium working in secret to restore what our betrayers tried to destroy. That's what you see here. Not those megalomaniacal fools who would only create their own form of the Houses, but the *real* Guardians, still alive and still fighting after all these years." He regards us both. "And I would like you to join us."

I don't know what to say. I want to claim I don't know these people, but it's not true. They've repeatedly saved my life. They just got done saving Amar's.

And if they really want to stop the Houses…

"We are up against a sociopath, a murderer, and a psychic, all rolled into one," Katsuro says. "And there's no telling what she's going to do next. But beyond even that, we have a greater issue. Magic is shifting, as I told you that night in the salvage yard. The convergence is coming, a magical event not seen in this world for a thousand years. Last time, the upheaval it caused gave rise to the Houses. This time, who knows what will occur? But the world *is* changing. The leaders of the Houses know this. I believe Penny does as well. All of them are searching for any strategy, any resource to give them an advantage amid what is to come. And that includes you two."

His mouth tightens. "There is hope, however. It is my opinion that Penny wanted you dead—*both* of you— because you are a threat to her and because you have a role to play in the coming days that she would prefer you not undertake. Now, you could face that on your own if that is your choice. You could run, hide, whatever you deem the best course. We will not stop you. But the convergence *is* coming, and the shift it will cause in this world has the potential for incredible harm. In light of that, I believe that the Guardians would benefit from your assistance to prevent Penny or the Houses from further destroying our world—and that *you* would benefit from our assistance to keep you both alive."

From the corner of my eye, I see Amar glance at me, and my heart jumps, reading the reluctance I glimpse on his face. He doesn't want me involved. He's the one who nearly *died*, and he's concerned about keeping me out of the line of fire. "I did this," I say, not quite looking at him. "I set Penny loose."

Amar shakes his head. "You couldn't have known she—"

My eyes find him this time, and he falls silent. "I knew something was wrong. I didn't know *what*, but—" My heart pounds. I'm aware of what I'm admitting: that Katsuro and everyone else is right. I really am like my mother. I have her powers too. "She terrified me. You both saw it. I knew."

I look up at Katsuro. "I'm in. What do we need to do?"

Katsuro pauses, glancing at Amar. "In that case, may I assume—"

"Yeah," Amar interrupts. "I'm in too."

Katsuro nods. "Then the first thing we do is simple—and potentially very difficult. In order to stop this revenge Penny has promised, and to keep her from hurting anyone else as well, we have to find her." He grimaces briefly. "Wherever she is."

19

KYLE

IN THE SMALL HOURS OF THE NIGHT, KYLE'S GREATEST SOURCE of comfort was the thought of all the people he'd eventually get to kill.

Ordinarily, anyway.

An angry sigh escapes him, and he glares up at the embossed tiles of the ceiling. He'd had Cait. Had that tall, dark, and handsome prick Amar too. The whole thing had been falling into place like a child's puzzle, and then…

Who the fuck had those demons been?

He punches the pillow under his head, trying in vain to make the feathers arrange themselves comfortably. His agents never mentioned Cait had help. Nothing like *that*, anyway. The Chastain family, sure. A few mercenary wolves as well.

But *that*…

He shifts on the silk sheets. This has practically put him back at square one. Worse, even. For all he knows, that Legacy bitch will tell that Legacy bastard about the coup, and next thing he knows, Lucretia's goons will be pounding down his door.

Awesome.

The door latch clicks in the quiet. He freezes for a heartbeat, his incredulity warring with his alarm, and then he's moving, out of the bed, across the room for the nearest line of shadow to get him the hell out of here.

"Uh-uh," chides a girlish voice.

He stops. Lights flare to life all around his enormous bedroom, and suddenly, he finds himself staring down the barrel of a gun.

A gun being wielded by a redheaded teenage girl.

His confusion grows.

She grins. "Hey there."

His gaze darts around the room. No one else has appeared. Nothing has changed. "Who are you? How did you get in here?"

The girl chuckles. "Oh, you can do better than that, Kyle."

He freezes. "How do you know my name?"

"I saw it," she replies like it's blatantly obvious. "I see so *many* things. Like you, helping me."

"And why would I do that?"

"Because I ask you to, silly."

The words are nonsense. His brow draws down warily. "Who are you?"

"I'm Penny." Her grin broadens. "How'd you like to rule the world?"

ABOUT THE AUTHOR

Skye Malone writes action-packed fantasy and paranormal romance. A fan of magical books since childhood, they adore stories that pit ordinary characters against extraordinary odds and reveal the strength within. Abandoned buildings are their passion, along with old castles and deep, dark parts of the forest where anything is possible. A graduate of the University of Illinois with a degree in English literature, Skye lives in the Midwest with a retired racing greyhound and a three-legged mutt.

ACKNOWLEDGMENTS

I owe tremendous gratitude to the many people who assisted me in the creation of this book.

Many thanks go to my mother and sister for their love, care, and unending support. Thank you both. I'm so grateful you're in my life.

To my dear friend, the talented proofreader Robin Augsburg, thank you for your help with my many grammar questions, and for being my friend.

Thank you to my fellow author and friend, Sara Whitney, for beta-reading this book and for her great suggestions for this series. I truly appreciate you.

To Veronica, the sensitivity reader from Salt and Sage, thank you. Thank you for your time, your energy in reading and making recommendations, and all the great insight you provided. I am very grateful for you. Many thanks as well to Erin Olds, owner of Salt and Sage, who coordinated communications between us, who handled logistics of sending files back and forth, and who does it all with a beautifully friendly and encouraging attitude.

Thank you to the gifted authors of my local RWA chapter for their input, advice, and insight. Thank you as well to my reader group on Facebook for their support. You all are amazing.

And last but certainly not least, thank YOU. Thank you for your time in reading, and thank you for buying this book. You make this wild and wonderful author-career thing possible.